THE OTHER WOMAN I AM

Also by GENEVIÈVE GENNARI

THE RIVEN HEART

THE OTHER WOMAN
I AM

By GENEVIÈVE GENNARI

Translated from the French
by LINDA ASHER

DAVID McKAY COMPANY, INC.

New York

THE OTHER WOMAN I AM

I felt frightened for the first time only when I sat down by the radio, and set the dinner tray on my knees.

And yet I had been through the worst of it. People are wrong when they say that the first shock of a grief is blunted by its very violence, and that one only starts to feel the pain later. People are often wrong—there are so many proverbs that need renovation, so many pieces of supposed wisdom that need re-examining! At the very instant I learned of Joseph's death, I felt the full weight of my grief. That lasted only a few seconds, fortunately. Any longer would have been unbearable. When I recovered consciousness I was no longer the same person. I was Joseph's widow; that I had understood. In a way I had even accepted it (for, unhappily, I had been expecting it). I began to weep without pain, by reflex, as one would hand a glass of water to a thirsting man. I thought vaguely, Jo will be pleased—remembering how amazed he had been that I had cried neither at my small daughter's death nor at my father's. "You know I haven't the gift for tears, Jo," I had told him again and again, but he had gazed at me uncomprehendingly.

To his mind, a woman is given the gift of tears at her birth, like a second baptism.

Only Jean-Christophe's presence carried me through the barbarous test of the funeral and of the family dinner afterward—that meal where everyone exposes his cannibal appetite, in the strict sense of the word. The food they devour so avidly is the corpse itself, that invisible but very present body, like the one in the surrealistic play that Jo had disliked (perhaps by some premonition)—that giant body stretched on the table, which would swell till it engulfed you, if it were not devoured first.

Afterward, with Jean-Christophe tending me, it was as though I were convalescing. He forced me to eat. I would have swallowed bayonets for him, as the saying goes; I ate. And in the street I leaned on him. "No one would ever take you for my mother," he would say, and I believed him. No, not really. All mothers seem young now; but still they are clearly the mothers of their sons.

He stayed with me six weeks; then I spent the summer in Corsica, at my mother's home. I put off my return to Paris as long as I could, wondering in anguish how I would stand Joseph's absence in that apartment; it is less than six months since he died. Here. Now I know that it will be hard. I managed to eat nothing off my tray; I rose and went down into the street, walking hard for a long while, racing against obsession; I pulled ahead and it floated behind me for a moment. Finally I slowed my steps; I was alone again, without memory.

Without Joseph.

It was wine-harvest weather under the October trees. I was soft and round, a ripe fruit fallen from a branch, bouncing lightly on the ground. Distance, weight had stopped existing. I was no longer completely myself. I was a fruit, a flower—

That sailor looked like Jean-Christophe, sitting there on the bench, with a fragile Vietnamese girl in silken pants. They had no need to speak: the impalpable vibration of the air was their voice; *they* were the fruit and the flower. I turned home, the giddiness gone. I was a widow but I had to eat—I must absolutely eat something. I picked up the tray again. The noodles were cold.

The last time I ate from a plate on my knees was six months ago in Chicago, and that day Joseph and I argued in public for the first time in our lives. There was nothing to warn me that two weeks later he would be dead. . . .

I had not considered myself happy; now I see the power of the feeling that bound me to Jo. There had been no love between us for—perhaps twenty years; but there was that tacit and irreplaceable habit that binds even a couple like us, who got along only on the condition of remaining silent on the essential questions.

According to well-established tradition, I am doomed to eternal remorse for what wrongs I may have done, and I am ashamed that already I feel less—oh, of course, I still feel remorse, but it is not so unbearable now as it was a few months ago. Why should I close my eyes to the humiliating truth? If Joseph came alive again, I would behave exactly the same way from that very instant. While he lived, I was always aware of what I had sacrificed for his sake. I sometimes felt that he had set himself like a screen between me and the immeasurable richness of the world, and that I was stifling in his shadow; I felt as if freedom and light began beyond that shadow. With

5

Joseph dead, though, it seems to me that he was the single bond that held me to the heart of things—that he was the natural bridge or intermediary between myself and the good things of this earth; and I feel myself cut off now from the stream of life. But I cannot bring myself to think of the dead Joseph as a barrier thrown down, any more than I could see the living Joseph as an intermediary. In both cases I am right. Or maybe wrong. It is the same story with any human relationship. Yet, if the Fontaines knew how thoroughly beaten I am, they would probably tell me what one of my sisters-in-law has already said to my friends the Höberlins—and what they cruelly repeated to me—that I *deserved* to be a widow!

Naturally, when I stand off to consider the woman I was six months ago; when I watch her climb the stairs to the Pan-American plane; when I recall how I took it for granted that I should be invited to the United States with Joseph, who was representing France at an engineering conference; when I remember that stay in Chicago which was to be—I couldn't have known—Joseph's last professional triumph; then, of course, I, too, am tempted to blame myself because I was not happy for one moment during that trip. But while I was living those moments, it was very different. Then I did not see them in relation to my present state, in relation to death—there was no reason to. Even objectively, that conference was a very dull series of days. In Chicago: endless speeches on technical subjects, and whisky. In Washington: champagne at the embassy under Bonaparte's portrait, and speeches. Speeches again in New York, in the women's club where we drank "to peace"—but there it was a glass of water. We never even visited a museum. But it was not really the museums I regret; museums are like warehouses. I should like to see the paintings free, back in their natural habitat: the Da Vincis in church, *La Goulue* in a café, the Salvador Dalis in an insane asylum.

What I wanted to do in America was to visit the Negro sections—reread Faulkner in Faulkner country—explore the great wild continent—inhale the smells of the South—and sail down the Potomac on the brightly lighted boat I had seen set off one night, teeming with young girls dancing barefoot on the deck. It was really not worth going all that way to swig champagne and hear speeches.

And I was so near.... My closest friend, a hostess for a Canadian air line, lived in Montreal, and I had not seen her for five years. The day before our last I had not yet given up hope; we could get to and from Montreal in twenty-four hours and be back in Chicago in time for the official farewell ceremony. It could be done if that day's luncheon finished early enough.

I was terribly bored during that luncheon of learned men. I could not exchange a word with their wives—I don't speak English—but while the men talked together on one universal topic, the Russian threat, I sensed the equally universal one the women were discussing: the impossibility of finding suitable domestic help. I tried to broach the Negro problem with the only one who spoke French, but Joseph turned his look on me—that gelid, glassy look that I called his fish eye. (Did I really call it that? Yes, my God, I did, and I will have to live with that memory.) I had borrowed the term from Sartre, who speaks of the "jelly-fish eye" of people who *reread* instead of reading, which was exactly what Joseph had come to do. I said no more.

A plate teetered unsteadily on my knees; on the floor between my feet I gripped a glass of California wine. As I cut awkwardly into my slice of turkey I thought, Wherever he

7

goes he rebuilds his cell, he secretes his shell everywhere...
wherever he turns that eye, life goes sterile.

As the afternoon drew on, I reminded him that my last
chance to see Irina hung by a hair—we should have to leave
immediately. This time he pretended not to hear, and even
avoided my glance. Joseph does not like Irina, and I know too
well his reason for not liking her. We started to argue in low
voices at first. When I muttered, "You have the advantage
because you're the one who's drawing the dollars. If I had
any money I'd leave right now," I saw him lose control of
himself for the first time. We quarreled, in front of everyone,
and suddenly they all grew silent as if to listen to us.

Joseph was the only one who seemed embarrassed; all the
others outdid each other in kindness, putting our nervous
irritation down to fatigue. And when we left, the hostess kissed
me on the mouth.

"That lunch was so heavy," was all Joseph said to me.

I did not mention Irina again. We made our peace treaty,
so to speak, in the hotel bed that evening. We always ended
by reconciliation. I shall not forget those nighttime truces,
weary and illusionless, like the handclasps of ancient and loyal
adversaries agreeing on a night's armistice.

This is what I think about, as I dine alone beside my radio,
and the thousand needles of remorse work into me. Yes, I
should like to be in Chicago again, six months ago; yes, I
should like to tell Joseph that I am happy and that I care for
him; I never said those things. I owed him everything, and
because I no longer loved him, I thanked him for nothing. I
cannot recall a single gleam of joy in his eyes. Of course I know
that the war, defeat, prison had broken him, had changed him

8

forever, and that indifference had become the very foundation of his nature. But still, twenty years ago I did kindle that look. ... It's all over, and I already know what old men know: that each experience may be unique, that each instant is sacred, and that the secret I sought so desperately behind things, when I still thought myself young enough to find it, may not exist.

Since I lost Joseph, all that I have lived seems ended as if I, too, had died. Till now my life was at once enclosed and infinite. It was a sphere rolled up on itself. It was the highway you speed along in a car, with the implicit confidence that it goes on around the world. And then the car stops, and the road takes on the realness of an object enlarged under a microscope —that spot on the road where you had the breakdown, the blowout, the fatal accident. Sometimes I used to imagine the trips we would take when we were older, a cottage on the banks of the Loire, the good calm of old age. But there would be none of that. All there was, was Chicago. There would only be Chicago, ever. My allotment of America in this life ... I would not have ten days of China. Would I even have ten days of Greece? Shall I learn English or Hebrew? Will I see the Paris catacombs and the *Third Man* sewers in Vienna? Will anyone ever send me an orchid?

And my allotment of love in this world will have been Jo, and I did not know how to profit by it, or to make it eternal. Three or four years of happiness, and almost twenty years of duty. And now how many years of regret, and of remorse on dark days?

I lowered my eyes to the tray and saw that I had eaten nothing. Suddenly I was afraid that I might never be able to eat again. That holiday hunger—a hunger so violent it is like desire—shall I never have to satisfy it again? I threw away the

9

leftovers—practically the whole meal—and carried down the garbage myself so as not to horrify Madame Bouquet, the cleaning woman who comes each morning. When I came back up and I saw our large double bed, I felt a chill. I stood beside it; aloud I asked Joseph's pardon for the past. I pulled the spread back up over the immaculate sheets and it felt as though I were shrouding a secret with my own hands.

I'll sleep in Jean-Christophe's old room where the bed is my size, a boy's bed.

Fortunately, I start work soon. On the level which I give the magnificent heading of the "sordid," Joseph took everything with him. His position allowed us to live well, but we had hardly been able to save. His car belonged to the plant. In a week I start as head saleswoman at a small fashion house run by my friend Marion Rapp.

I have so often resented my inability to show people that I was not simply Madame Fontaine—to remind them that I once had ambitions for a life of my own, and toward what have to be called convictions, laughable as it seems. Now the time has come when I can—when I must—match those convictions to my actions. It is probably only fair that I should pay such a heavy price for it.

Many people would be surprised to learn that there exists a woman—myself—who suffered from the fact that her husband held different beliefs from her own. But they should actually be more surprised that this is one of the only topics that women politicians never bring up, and one of the few motives that a divorce trial never mentions. There are always the same little sentimental complications, always the same physical incompatibility, or the quarrels of financial interest.

Never that great pure cry that I would have raised if I had had the courage to fight Joseph by words, by arguments and acts rather than by my niggardly everyday discontent.

"It's your opinions I cannot share, it is because of what's best in me that I no longer love you!" What I call the best in me is the personal vocation that I had as a young girl; it is the interest I always felt in political battles, in the world's future—it is my reasoned, and paradoxically almost carnal, passion for freedom of mind; it is my desperate quest for truth. But I was always painfully aware that my case was unusual. That a man and woman should be unsuited, at least to some degree, because they have different opinions—isn't that extraordinary? Mightn't we be the only such case there is? In any event, the very strangeness of my situation helped me to gauge the state of indifference in which most women live, when it comes to problems of the human condition.

Politics is a tradition in my family—my father was deputy from Corsica; my great-great-grandfather one of Paoli's lieutenants. And my cousin Augustin Costa has dedicated his life to founding a French labor party. But I do not limit the definition of the word "convictions" to the political sense; I include in it all the religious aspiration, the philosophic ferment, the individual morality of a man. A political attitude is only meaningful as part of a whole. Nothing reveals a being better than his convictions or his lack of them.

So I was Bonapartist till eighteen, or for as long as I was under the exclusive influence of my parents. But even then, even much younger, the past interested me only because it held the germs of the future; as ridiculous as it seems today, for me the future of France was Napoleon IV. I registered at the École des Sciences Politiques with the intention of going into politics later. Very soon I began to fear that I was a regime or two too late. When I finished school, I no longer had any longing to work for a lost cause; I wanted to campaign for the women's vote. But already I felt divided against myself. . . . When I was small, my parents used to say I had the mind of a boy. It seems incredible now. And later Mother would tell me, "Be more girlish. You're not feminine enough. No man is going to want you if you keep announcing you want to be a deputy, and keep your own family name stuck onto your husband's!" I was afraid she might be right.

And then I married as soon as I finished school. I married because I loved Jo Fontaine, very simply, and I did what girls of my class did at the time: I gave up the idea of any professional activity, any intellectual investigation. Then I was sure I had gone completely feminine! And to emphasize it the more I spoke of my studies, and of my old ambitions, as I would of the attack of piety we all go through at twelve or fifteen, complete with dreams of the cloister. I would speak of it ironically, as of a period forever gone. The Fontaines belonged to Action Française, they were anti-Semitic, ultramontane, and so forth. Their only dilemma was choosing between Charles Maurras and the Pope. But I didn't want to think about that; I was twenty, I loved Jo, and I was happy. Those are the things that count, aren't they? Then I had Jean-Christophe, and I learned that the passion of motherhood could be more violent and more tender than the passion between man and woman.

The war came two years later. And that is when it all started.

We still loved each other when Jo left in 1939. We loved each other no longer when we met again in 1945. It seems to be a sadly common story, and for the Fontaines I am the very prototype of the morally faithless prisoner's wife. But no—it's not so banal as that.

For six years I was alone. From 1939 on I had begun again to think for myself, I had taken some courses again, met Irina, and rediscovered friendship and freedom. And then, most important, I had discovered in 1940 that my father, a deputy, whom I admired; my engineer husband, whom I still believed I loved; and the immense majority of my teachers had been as completely mistaken as men could be. We had come to the end of an age, a new one was beginning, and none of them had foreseen it. Without the war, that six-year separation, and our development in opposite directions, I might never have noticed that Joseph and I were not made for each other. But 1940 was, for me as for a great many people, the essential break; 1940 was a refutation of everything France had been, everything my own people had told me, everything I had believed.

From that time on I have never been the same. In a certain unclear way I felt responsible for a disaster that I myself had not foreseen either. I was obsessed by Dostoyevsky's words: Everyone is responsible for everything, to everyone.

On the exodus roads I clutched a little three-year-old boy to me and if he had been killed I would have died. What am I saying! If Jean-Christophe had died, I would have killed myself. I swore then that I would never again believe in a truth without staring its reverse full in the face. I did not want Jean-Christophe to experience a collapse like mine in his future, and to be able to reproach me one day with having misled him. I made a choice then. Then I came to understand, through the enormous error of my father and of my husband, what can never be forgotten: that any part truth is a lie.

Afterward I battled alone for five years to see that my son was well nourished and warm. In the chaos that followed the disaster I was totally alone again. Irina was in London, my husband in East Prussia, my parents in Corsica. I quarreled with the Fontaines; they worshiped Marshal Pétain as a god, and Laval as his prophet, and spoke of General de Gaulle (whom they called Gaulle) as the Antichrist. To have been wrong once was not enough for them; with the insane light-heartedness of "those whom the gods would destroy" they had transferred onto Greater Germany a little of their disappointed French passion.

If I had not had the entire responsibility for my son, I would have gone into the Resistance. (I learned later, too late, that my cousin Augustin had covered the Costa name with glory in the movement....) Not only out of patriotism—oh, no! For liberty above all. And for beauty as well.... I had taken over the old British motto: "For England and for beauty." For England or for France, for Finland or for China, because we have to. But for beauty, above all, because we don't have to, for freedom because it is the greatest beauty and the most neces-sary one. In any event, I had decided that when the war was over I would ponder with Joseph on our own particular prob-lems and on the general drama; I would take up some activity; in short, start my life again on new foundations. My discov-eries came one after another, at a speed that dizzied me: I was no longer in love with my husband, my country had shriveled like a prune skin, and my learning had been nothing but a sterile game. What giddiness, what an awakening! I was still staggering from it when Joseph came home.

I was hoping for a miracle—it is my nature to believe in miracles. I was twenty-nine years old; I had a conqueror's soul and a body that had waited six years to live. On the ruins of a love between two beings who were too young, and probably too romantic, I hoped to rebuild something more austere but stabler, too. It took almost no time to see that our schism was more serious than I had feared.

Oh, I know he had his problems, too; I know that he needed to come home to the young girl in love, the feminine little bride he had left behind; and I was no longer that. He needed to come back to a wife who still loved him blindly, and in whose eyes he could find a reassuring image of himself as something else than a conquered man. Beliefs, the ideal, his country—they had been important for him, too, and he must have felt a collapse like mine. But, unlike me, he wanted neither to recognize it nor to take the consequences.

Fundamentally, he had changed in a direction opposite to mine. Or, more precisely, he had not changed at all; he had changed no more than if he were returning from a long vacation. Yet something had happened, because the tall, slim, blond boy I had loved had become that melancholy and bitter man; because his blue gaze had grown rigid; and because he would never again say "I love you" ... For he never told me again that he loved me either after his return. Nor did our bodies recognize each other when they met. I shall never know which disillusionment, the physical or the moral, brought about the other.

And still—even in this shipwreck—if he had been willing to accept the fact that I was no longer the person he had left behind, as I was prepared to do toward him; the fact that I was a thirty-year-old woman who had lived alone, had raised a child, and ripened her thoughts, perhaps.... But this, too, was a part of the new Joseph: to deny all change, never again to face squarely any difficulties he could avoid. His eye no longer adjusted. In a sense, Joseph, too, had died in 1940, and his story was the story of a whole social class. The young idealistic bourgeois, the charming young man in love, capable of enthusiasm—he existed no more. There remained only a tired man now, an intellectual soured by the discovery (and the denial) of his own mistakes, a scientist who would henceforth refuse to consider the slightest problem outside his field. In prison he had reread, studied, and annotated all of Balzac. He would never do anything now but reread. His mind had been so alert and curious, and he had adopted this old man's phrase at forty: "At my age, one no longer reads ; one rereads." He hoped for nothing more now than intellectual comfort, the maintenance of categories and traditions. His irony (which was also new) could be maddening, and I feared it more than the—very masculine—force of inertia which he set against whatever might threaten his internal comfort. Another strange thing: little by little he developed a worldliness, a slight snobbery; he spent greater and greater attention on the refinements of his clothing. I should probably have understood that this behavior betrayed his need to believe in the still-intact forms of what had been his way of life, in what survived of the class that was declining along with him. Aside from his profession, which demanded that he always be a step ahead of things, he was—I told him this often enough to have the courage to repeat it to myself—Joseph was narrow-minded.

As soon as I mentioned my plans to him, I saw how deeply I wounded him—in his husbandly pride, in his convictions as a man, and in what tenderness he still felt for me. I did not

want to go too far, I wanted to save what could be saved between us, and I gave him the sole proof of femininity in my
power: I voluntarily gave up the idea of starting on a career
that my father could have helped me with then. My opinions
had become so different from Jo's that my project would have
meant betrayal to him. Soon the joy of awaiting another child,
the greatest of all joys to me, made me forget the new flare of
ambition. But my small daughter did not live, and with a
single-minded passion I threw myself again toward Jean-
Christophe.

Later, when I saw Jean-Christophe learning history from a
book that looked like the one I had had twenty years earlier,
and learning the Code of Honor from Corneille, I reminded
him that there were six hundred million Chinese, and that he
would have to live and think on a world scale. I told him that
if we try to move ahead of a development rather than follow
it, we can be sure to make no mistakes, and that choosing the
future is the only choice that cannot be wrong. But I was
wrong; my son is not Chinese, luckily! And the world is too
big for us to ask a child to grow up to its scale. Joseph recited
Péguy and Hugo's *Châtiments* to him, and told him tales of
his poor little war that had lasted ten months—never of his
imprisonment that had lasted five years. He was proud of belonging to a family of the authentic Parisian bourgeoisie (they
are very rare, of course, those bourgeois of Paris who date
from Charles V and who may bear the reliquary of Saint
Geneviève); he would recite him the history of the Fontaine
family, a history far more illustrious than the Costas'. And
when I read a newspaper other than his, he would smile to his
son, and say, "Your mother is like all women who are inter-

ested in politics—an idealist," and his indulgent tone made it clear that he considered me harmless.

I did not answer. I never answered. I wanted Jean-Christophe to be able to choose between us, freely. When Joseph, always smilingly, would call me a progressive or a feminist, I could not help but find those ridiculous words beautiful, and I hoped Jean-Christophe would feel it, too. But I could not tell him what I thought: that his father's rigidity of attitude betrayed a certain internal weakness, a new lack of curiosity; I could not tell him that I thought his father narrow-minded. Those are hard words to say about a man who can explain the secrets of nuclear fission and guided missiles.

And Jean-Christophe did choose freely. Neither his father's side nor mine. No side at all. Jean-Christophe has the good luck neither of us had: a basic, almost organic happiness. More artist than intellectual, he has no interest in politics; he has an instinctive faith in men because his own heart is true. Through his own body he senses the world as harmony; he believes in God as naturally as he loves music. He inherited his curiosity about the future from me, but he has the active form: he is fascinated by horizons and new lands, by travels and the exotic. At eighteen Jean-Christophe entered a colonial school in Marseilles. Last year he was engaged to Nadine, and they are communicants together at the altar of youth.

Jean-Christophe's presence had been enough to keep me happy. Times are still good in a home where a man and a woman share the same child and own him entirely. And then Jean-Christophe left.

I was never stronger, I never looked younger than at that time. Irina says that after they have raised their children,

American women go back to work, at the age of thirty-five or forty; I was at that age when I wanted to for the first time. Not only did I feel I had become useless, but somehow I felt it unnatural to take money from Joseph for the household, or for my clothes, once Jean-Christophe had left us. When I heard myself saying, "Please, Jo, I'd like to have thirty thousand francs to finish out the month," my face burned. It burned when I read his tax return—number of *dependents*: 2. I had reason to flush; I no longer had reasons for being dependent on my husband. But when I told him I had decided to work, he smiled ironically.

"And who would hire you at your age, silly? There are plenty of causes that need volunteer help, if you're interested in social problems."

"No," I said, "I want to do real work—earn a little money, feel some independence."

I wanted to explain, to make him understand, but all I could do was recite a speech that seemed childish. I listed rather literary reasons, I see that; I repeated sentences that I had rehearsed beforehand, about the need women have for some outside expression of their personality, and so on. . . . Then he cut in, his smile gone, with his soft-spoken firmness:

"You've always known that to me a wife means a wife in the home. I cannot forbid you, but I ask you to give up this whim. Because that's all it is, isn't it?" he ended.

It seems to me now that I surrendered very quickly. But I was forty years old. And probably, deep in my heart, I felt my life was over.

Thus I have spent these last three years doing voluntary work for a public library, and I devoted the rest of my time to managing my house. It brought an easy way to forget; in every woman there is a hidden homemaker. Oh, and what a good homemaker she was, that Sylvestre Costa who had dreamed of going to parliament! Joseph took greater and greater pleasure in entertaining, and his guests were more and more important people. At old Albine's side I relearned the secret of those metamorphoses that only seem matter-of-fact after long habit: sugar that hardens to caramel, the fluid egg that congeals into a yellow-and-white eye. . . . I haunted sales-rooms; I gave parties and strained my imagination to make them unusual. I sprayed the electric-light bulbs before lighting them, so that the scent of my own perfume would rise from them; I gave Russian, Italian, Chinese dinners. The most successful was the Hebrew dinner: in a bookstall I found the volume of a slightly insane Englishwoman who had put together a manual of ritual cuisine drawn from the Bible, and I bought a seven-branched candlestick for the centerpiece.

Joseph and I lived in silence.

I had no absolute doctrine, no definitively closed opinion. My father had died and I had no longer any connection with circles which Joseph so deliberately avoided. But I would so have liked to seek truth, with or without him. . . . It was then —and again for the same reasons—then I began to ask myself agonizing questions on various points of my religion, to study the history of the Reformation, of the orthodox church, of the heresies. I was no longer a "practicing" Catholic except to accompany Joseph. I subjected everything to re-examination, and this deepened still farther the abyss that separated me from my husband. What pained me most was that he did not believe that my search was torment to me. He never mentioned it, except to quote Pascal: "Make yourself stupid"; but it was clear that he considered all my anguish—social, political, or religious—as self-indulgence on my part, an intellectual game, while I felt myself lashed to the rack. Only someone who has lived through a crisis like mine can know how terrible a trial it can be—a train of thought capable of bringing a papist, nationalist, colonialist, and conformist little Frenchwoman to the point of submitting everything to question.

Out of curiosity, once last spring in Chicago, I leafed through a popular history book displayed in a drugstore. I looked automatically for the word "France" . . . I knew enough English, anyway, to understand the few thunderous words that summed up 1940: "The most ignominious defeat in the world." I had thought myself cured long before; but it was as though I were being stabbed once again. "Jo, look!" I said. He let his indifferent gaze slide over it. "Yes, I see. But that's ancient history. . . ." And for once he was the one who was right. Unhappily, we were never right at the same time.

But if I could not tell my husband, whom could I tell how much I suffered at not reading the same papers as he, at having an opposite opinion to his on so many subjects, at not being able to talk with him about the problems that interested me most? There was Indochina, then Europe, then the worker-priests—there was always Franco or Algeria—and we never had the same viewpoint.

Everyone understands it when two brothers, and even two comrades in arms, reach the point of lifelong enmity over such questions, because people sense vaguely what essential values are involved in them; but who would have believed that an apparently united couple could be split for the same reasons? Everyone forgot that I had been raised in the din of parliamentary discussions, and that my father treated his daughter as an equal, with her mind like a boy's. But I was not thinking with a mind like a man's. It was I as a woman, as my whole self—I felt at issue. But a woman with ideas of her own, in Joseph's world, was a monster; amusing, but a little monster all the same.

So Joseph "reread," and I—I tried to put myself gently back to sleep, to anesthetize myself. It was not unpleasant, and I often thought I had managed to do it. I spent time with the Fontaines again, to please Jo. I spent entire months at the estate Joseph's uncles owned at Neuves, in Deux-Sèvres—an isolated, uncomfortable house where Great-uncle Fontaine imposed an atmosphere like the one Chateaubriand knew at Combourg. Joseph liked staying there, because of his acquaintances in the neighborhood and because of the hunting; and I was bored with the fervor one usually expends on enjoying oneself.

But I had learned to assent to it all for whole days at a time, without its even bothering me. Occasionally I would suddenly even feel at home, adopted, as though I had been naturalized or annexed to another France—a circle so tradition bound that the conversations would often turn to the Vendée war, and immediately make it seem closer than World War II; in a region so religious that it was the lay teacher who had no pupils and who figured as the pariah. There is a repressed royalist in every Frenchman, and I am no exception to the rule: my youthful Bonapartism is the proof of it. At Neuves I would sometimes drowse off into the great sweetness of a dream of the past. And there I met women with names like Isaure or Ségolène—so blond, so Frankish that I felt I should explain my small stature and my black hair by reminding them that I was Corsican. Good Lord, how feminine they were, those women, when the evening came and, all fragrant with sun lotion or with Guerlain, they would welcome their husbands home from the tractor or the hunt. I thought sadly that this was the kind of girl Joseph should have married. Until later, in our room, when he found the magazines and the papers that I bought almost clandestinely in the village, he would smile protectively and say, "Silly little woman!"—the words that always signaled our reconciliations.

Joseph liked most to entertain his foreign friends at Neuves, too; I have never understood how they could all look so much alike—the ones I had met in Paris and in Chicago, and the ones who would spend a few days at Neuves, on their way from Frankfort or Palermo, to Spain or the Riviera.

They are engineers, yet they do not seek out the secret of the Numbers. They reread Dante, Shakespeare, or Chateaubriand, but none of them has read Marx, not even to try to refute him. They have all undergone defeat, many have known shame or invasion; yet they are not devoting their lives to finding out the cause. Worse still: they never think about the war that is taking shape, nor of ways to prevent it. (I think about it a lot; I think about it all the time. Along with cancer and the afterlife of the soul it seems to me the only subject worthy of interest, from America to China. I think about it because of Jean-Christophe, but also because of everyone in the world.) They are generally good Christians, but if you were to ask them their ideas on the transcendence of God, none of them could answer.

They have all gone through the Flood and they have stayed the same. I have never understood how people can take possession of the earth again so placidly. Jean-Christophe grew up after the deluge; thank you, my God, for giving him the un-awareness of the new age and of the new earth. But I—when I was twenty-five I saw the sky burst open, and I still feel beneath my feet the subterranean surge of the waters.

So many times, in the midst of a dinner or a walk, I wanted to cry "Wake up! A billion humans are slowly dying of hunger in China and in India. Soon they will come to wrench open your Frigidaires, and smash your Renaults and your Volkswagens and your motor scooters! Wake up, there are six hundred million Chinese! Twice you have been late for your appointments with history—do you want it to happen again? Here you are, afraid that Russia may come to disturb your comfort, while Russia is already fearful of the broom she gave the yellow sorcerers! Wake up! Have you read the Bible? Have you counted the stars?"

But I did not cry out. I accepted the glass of whisky, the champagne goblet. I smiled, I said "*Ja, ja*," "*Si, si*." Joseph was content to talk figures, and to think me content. Why should I have cried out? Or smashed my glass? I was not doing anything, either, to halt the march of hunger, or to feed the Chinese children; I, too, was profiting from the advantages that came from the accident of being born in a rich land. And when I read the Psalms, I do it, too, to lull myself with the measureless music of the words.

How many years is it since I recited the prayer of Tagore's that Irina taught me once, and that I had adopted? It rises to my lips again today:

There where the spirit is without fear and the head is carried high, there where knowledge is free,

24

... There where the spirit, with your guidance, advances
in the endless widening of thought and of action,
In that paradise of freedom, my Father, let my country
awaken!

For how long had I been asleep, clutching Joseph's arm, like
a sleepwalker on a parapet? His death has awakened me, and
I have no more parapet. I am suspended over the void.

For the past six months I have been sustained only by the
will to work. I count the days, the hours, that still lie between
me and the day I start at the Maison Rapp.

I shall not be working at Marion Rapp's salon.

She phoned me this morning, asking me to come see her; it
was urgent. She was waiting for me in her little gray-and-gold
salon on the Rue Saint-Honoré, perched on the old desk, and
at first I did not understand why her husband was there with
her. Actually, I know them very little; they are just tennis-
court friends. They are both much younger than I; Marion is
tall and blond, still terribly young-deb despite her two children and her fashion house; Pierrot plays the avant-garde de-
signer, and always wears a black turtleneck sweater.

On the outside, the building oozes with the grime of two
hundred years. But indoors at the Rapps' all is fresh and newly
painted. I already felt at home. . . . In that setting Pierrot in
his eternal pullover looked like a masquerade burglar or the
heir to some foreign fortune.

"Marion is very fond of you," he began, "and I'd like to be
helpful in some way. Do you speak English, Sylvestre?"

"Marion knows that I don't," I answered, surprised.

"Even if they speak two languages," Pierrot said, emphasizing each word, "our saleswomen make only forty thousand francs, plus commission on the dresses they sell to their personal clients. Frankly," he finished, with a tone of false concern, "I'm wondering whether this work is worthy of you."

I was confused—"do you speak English?" ... not worthy of me ... In the past I had ordered one or two dresses from the Rapps, out of friendship. I had stood in this same office to pay my bill, horrified by the price asked for a dress as ephemeral as a flower, yet aware of the miracle that this brief and pure flowering represented, born of sweating hands amid hardheaded calculations. I wanted more intensely than ever to share in that weariness of which I had taken advantage earlier, as a client. I said resolutely: "I can try."

"No," Pierrot said. "A woman has to be very young to start in this business. You should have an important job in an older house. Around here they're young bohemians. We outfit the existentialist muses, once they've chopped off their pigtails!"

I nodded, "Yes—yes ..."

This time I understood. "A woman has to be very young." ... "An older house" ... And yet, one day in this same office, to encourage me to choose a certain dress, this same voice had said "You could really wear our junior line."

I waited impatiently for the end. Why hadn't I noticed how young they were? Scarcely thirty, a household of recent teenagers who ride to the tennis courts in a little Renault. Their two babies play with a big stuffed German tiger, and Marion watches them out of the corner of her eye, between volleys. Young Bohemia ... These children spend their lives between a car and the bathroom where they sleep at the workshop on the Place Blanche.

"You aren't angry with us?" Marion murmured when I rose.

That was the last thing she should have said. But I smiled; I said, "No, no," and I left. A kitchen on the mezzanine opens onto the eighteenth-century staircase; the smell of warmed-over food followed the perfume of the Rapp salon. I felt sick. Not only because I needed work, and because suddenly I did not know where to go for it, but because I felt the weakness of my position before the two Rapps; I felt terrifyingly ill-equipped, because I was the black-robed widow and they that triumphal pair. Probably at that moment he was consoling her: "Look, there was an abscess and it had to be lanced, darling. . . ." I was the abscess.

I had taken a taxi to go to Marion's. I took the Métro home.

It will not be as easy as I had imagined to take my life into my own hands. How could I ever have thought it would be easy? I don't deserve it.

I marvel now that everyone, all around me, seems to have a job, and seems always to have had one. I had never admired Joseph for being an engineer in a large plant at Puteaux; I should have. He was a graduate of the École Centrale, he had a war medal, he was nice-looking—it seemed his due. I had never asked him how he had found his job. Yes, I had been wrong. I lived in a world where everyone seemed to have his place. But my age, which I had never thought about, had fallen onto my back like an overcoat. Was its weight what was crushing me? I found that I was stooping a little.

Ever since I have been making it clear to my friends that I don't simply *want* to work, but that I *need* to work, I have

27

the impression that I am the first woman who ever asked them for it, and that I seem strange and incongruous to them. (What would they think if I borrowed money from them?) They all answer, "I'll give it some thought." None of them has the courage to tell me, "I shall certainly not give it a moment's thought." The only one who has actually promised to help me is my old enemy Georges Höberlin; he is a former classmate at Sciences Politiques, now a cabinet minister. We are bound by a tie stronger than love, stronger than friendship: an antipathy which has lasted faithfully over more than a quarter of a century. When he repeated my sister-in-law's terrible words —"She deserved to be a widow"—I may have been wrong in thinking he did it out of malice. Höberlin considers me so naïve, so unenlightened, as he says, that he thinks it more necessary and more decent to inform me of the painful realities.

Suddenly there is no longer a spot for me in this world where each person seems to have one reserved for him since birth with a number like a theater seat. I am outside the egg. This is not simply my impression. It is a fact. It is completely out of order that I, a typical middle-class woman, forty-three years old, and without skills, should want to work. I had some vague, unformed idea that at the root of the society we live in, supply and demand roughly coincide. But if I thought that the supply and the demand were so well balanced, that was probably because I was demanding nothing. It's not at all the same thing to take gratuitous interest in social problems, for their own sake, and to be faced with a vital need.

Since I have been reading the classified advertisements, for employment wanted or available, I see the whole clubfooted ballet of the stumblers dance before my eyes in black-and-white characters. It is the ballet of those who cannot find their way marked out before them, or who have lost it; of those who never walk with sure step, because they do not know where they are going, or because they are going nowhere: "Blind poet seeks young boy to sell poems door to door." . . . "Woman, sixty-nine years old, well preserved, seeks supervision lavatories, day or night." . . . "Retired senior officer would exchange apartment (three rooms) for steady work." It's worse than the matrimonial columns. Seeking love, hawking oneself through the press, is pitiable, and that can be touching. But he who seeks his bread . . . When I went to the office of my newspaper, to put in my own ad, there was a young Austrian girl with a moon face next to me. "I want my advertisement to appear tomorrow," she kept repeating. "It has to. Starting tomorrow."

"But you have no address to give me! I must have an address for my register," answered the clerk, and the clerk seemed invested with his role for all eternity, he seemed to have been born on that chair, like a crown prince on the steps of the throne. The Austrian girl finally gave "University of Paris" as her address, and the clerk was satisfied. Ritual performed.

I never had an answer to my own advertisement.

Jean-Christophe writes me from each port his ship touches. "Have you found work? It is absolutely necessary for your moral balance." I have been careful to hide from him the fact that from the "sordid" standpoint it is urgent. I insist on handling the situation by myself. I have simply sold my ring, and I can wait.

It is much more difficult than I had thought to sell one's jewels, one's furniture, one's dresses. Living by stopgaps is

29

almost a craft in itself. I let myself get into the spirit of the thing, and for a while it distracted me. But the excitement of victory has subsided now. I am safe from need for a few months, but the very urgency of that need at least masked the emptiness of my life. Now I have fallen into a bottomless tedium, like the well in bad dreams. Frankly, I must admit that I also miss the security that Joseph's presence gave me. I am not proud of myself, but there it is.

The simple fact of having had a husband seems a miracle to me, a very-long-ago miracle that occurred in one of my other lives. Yet everyone has a husband or a wife. Even Jean-Christophe will be married, in less than a year, at the end of his military service. But that is what is amazing—that so many things happen naturally and harmoniously, as though life, or a God, owed us that procession of miracles—youth and love, health, a home, and the hope of dying only from old age, like a tree.

In a sense we are trees, with our feet rooted in the earth, our faces lifted toward the stars, our arms stretched out like branches. Oh, vines of the Lord, Jesse's rod, cedars of Lebanon, oaks of Mamre, the just increase like the palm tree—I lived among miracles and I did not see it! I lived in Joseph's shadow, but also *by* his shadow, and the day I saw him laid on his deathbed, feet torn from the soil, arms folded, face closed—from the day when I saw him uprooted, I should have understood: I was henceforth the tree left standing alone after a tempest, prey to all the winds, on a battered, storm-struck hill.

Madame Bouquet will come only one day a week now, on Saturdays, and the trouble I take to keep up my apartment seems absurd. Waxing the floor for a widow's feet—what a farce! What dance does this fine inlay gleam for?

I must face the truth. I have lost the habit of seeking any justification for my existence, other than that of being Madame Joseph Fontaine, mother of Jean-Christophe. And Virginie's mother too, but for so short a time. . . .

We called her "The Prisoner's Return," the little girl I had a year after Joseph's liberation. But Prisoner's Return was born of parents who were too exhausted; she weighed five pounds and did not live. I never lost the longing for another child, but I did not have one.

Virginie would be twelve and a half now; she would be dark like me, she would have thick braids and her brother's blue eyes. . . . Perhaps everything would be different. A child does not compensate for a man or for a man's absence. But it justifies a woman. What am I saying? A mother no longer needs justification herself: she transfers her whole self into the living child.

I am alone in an apartment with bright walls, with light curtains, and suddenly the very luxury of cleanliness seems absurd. It is as though lovingly, unwittingly, I have prepared a tomb for myself.

Yet in Joseph's lifetime everything made sense. The thought obsesses me. Haven't I the right to live for myself alone? Ah— that's the whole question! Life is an absolute good. I should have the right to live without feeling myself guilty. But since Joseph's death I am ashamed when I buy myself flowers, when I open a bottle of old wine for my dinner, when I go to a movie alone. Why should I be ashamed? Then, too, I had leisure time, I filled it according to my whim, and I felt no shame.

31

I took courses at the Collège de France, I read magazines, I worked for that public library. Today I no longer have a taste for it. I have grown aware that those were the pastimes of idle people. My freedom is killing me.

To a Communist I might perhaps appear to be a condemnation of the regime we live under. Let us be cynical: I have lived like a parasite, cared for by my parents till the age of twenty, and by my husband from then on. Now I am at middle age, with the only attributes employers do not require: the education, the good manners, and the "respectable appearance" of the typical upper-middle-class woman.

Am I to be ashamed of the bread I eat? Saint Paul said that "if any would not work, neither should he eat." But what about those to whom no work is offered? And I cannot find work because until now I have been nothing but an integral part of a system—free only within the framework that contained me. Because I have no other worth than the one that cannot be measured, cannot be weighed: simply that of a human being, that of a woman. A woman who, I think for the first time, may have been in certain ways a happy one, despite everything and even unknown to herself.

Yet I must live. One has to live. I see everyone living. I mean that everyone seems to have a reason for living. . . . Not only the Rapps, with their happiness that makes me blink my eyes, like the sun. But my cleaning woman is a widow, too, and she lives. She divides her time with the rhythm of a metronome, and does not rest the whole day long. Madame Bouquet's dream is to save enough money to buy herself a car and become a taxi driver, like her late husband. It was she who said the hard words I never tire of musing over: "They should train all women to be widows—they are usually younger than their husbands, and they live longer."

Everyone lives. In the scenes framed by open windows I see families gather about their tables; climbing back to my apartment to swallow the noodles, the slice of ham, and the yoghurt that appear again each night on my tray, I smell the aroma clouding from the kitchens of all the apartments in my building, and from the concierge's, too. Materially speaking, that is perhaps the hardest for me: not to share in the warmth of the meal, to be deprived of that communion among stomachs which, nonetheless, I did not always love before.

Back in the time when I contemplated the problem from the outside, from the haven of a security that (God forgive me) I found dismal, I had some vague notion that it was the same thing to be a single woman and to be a free woman. But it is not at all the same thing. No, I do not feel free. I only feel alone. . . . When I became a widow, I promised myself to be as courageous as Irina. But I know already that I will not be so courageous: Irina has the new blood of a very young country in her veins—she was born the same year as Finland. What a symbol, to be born at the same time as one's country! Would I have the courage, myself, to wash dishes as she did for three months?

I admired Irina. I pitied my friend Paule du Haut-sur-Pas, a philosophy professor, who bears not only that difficult name, but also a spectacular ugliness that condemns her to solitude. But fundamentally I had no idea what it meant, in concrete terms, to "manage by oneself." And I did not know how much different things would look to me, and how I should have to learn all over again, through a whole series of new beginnings.

When you see a hunchbacked girl or a blind derelict pass,

33

you pity them. So do I. But we cannot imagine ourselves hunchbacked, or derelict, can we? At the most, we imagine somehow that if we were that humped girl, or that blind man, we would be another person, so different from ourselves that some mysterious strength would descend to help us bear our fate, as they say. But no. They suffer from their misfortune as we ourselves would suffer in their stead: intolerably. Thus it is not a new Sylvestre who sits alone before her radio, a platter on her knees; it is I myself, living, buried alive like the Roman vestals who broke their vows. It is I who perform the gestures of a living woman. It is I who open my arms and . . . I awake like a patient after surgery, and I find four amputated stumps.

To Marion I have become widowhood itself. She often telephones me, evenings: "You're not bored all alone?" she asks anxiously. "You're not feeling blue? Have you found work?" Marion is kind. But behind her I hear Pierrot's guitar, or the feverish noise that rises from the Place Blanche; I imagine the plate-glass showwindows, draped with a theatrical hanging of black satin, the square divan with four equal sides that fills the center of the workroom; and I imagine her stretched flat on her stomach, one leg waving her slim heel in the air. How could she guess that I was no more born a widow than she, that no mysterious strength has been granted me for my condition since I became one, that I suffer from it as much as she would, and that, for me, the injustice is that I am the widow and not she?

No! I don't want to become unfair. It may be true—the truth can be black—that I deserved my fate, since I never ceased to feel myself dissatisfied with Joseph, and because I always held it against him that he had not let me begin a career in 1945, or go to work ten years later.

Well, Sylvestre, here you are, free! Now it's up to you!

No, I shall not be unfair. But already I am forced to become calculating. Whatever good I have done, freely and with joy, now I measure it and set it down in disgust at myself. In disgust, but I do count it. All the small favors I have done I recall from the depths of the past; I weigh them; I measure them. My one evening dress I had ordered from Marion, when the fashion house was just starting, with some difficulty. Paule will always owe me something. Georges Höberlin has been a guest at my parents' house in Corsica several times. I can ask any of them a favor. But I still do not understand why it is I who am reduced to that, and not they.

Irina writes me a perfect letter from Montreal:

"You are living through the hardest time now. But soon you will be like a blind man recovering his sight: you will rediscover the world with your eyes and your heart. I understand that after a series of electroshock treatments the first time you go outdoors it feels as though you had stumbled onto the creation of the world. Well, when you have gotten over this shock, you will see that the world is waiting to be reborn until you come."

I think of Irina a great deal since I became a widow, and I have a tremendous desire to see her. Will it be another of the discoveries that my new condition holds in store for me? It seems to me that in the life of a married woman friendship is a superfluous thing. My friendship for Irina had become incomplete without my knowing it; only loneliness makes us entirely available, and for good reason.

When I met her in 1939, she was working at the Finnish

Legation and had just lost her fiancé, one of those legendary officers of the Russo-Finnish war. Joseph had been mobilized, and I was anxious and depressed. Some instinct made me apprehensive about the outcome of the war, and I joined a society of cosmic philosophy that claimed to know the secret of the future. It was there I met her. Irina was looking for some means of contact with the man she had loved.

In that sinister and unhealthy collection of cosmic philosophers her extreme youth, her eyes, and her pale hair shone with the sun's rays. We were quite naturally drawn to each other, and we quit the cosmic society to take courses together at the Sorbonne. That athletic girl had no trouble absorbing the French culture. I saw the ice melt little by little, and the white face take on life. She met an American diplomat and loved him because he was handsome.

No one would believe me if I stated this absolute truth: that before I met Irina I never knew that one could consider the flesh so naturally, and live its life so simply that ultimately one achieves greater detachment through satisfaction than through renunciation—and greater purification. I did not know that the same person could be a ski champion and know Rabindranath Tagore by heart, believe in phantoms, and have a pilot's license. I did not know that a woman can match a man in work. I even think that I no longer knew that man and woman are made one for the other: I had accepted the notion that woman alone was made for man, and I believed I had given up a personal life forever. It was a long time since I had thought about fighting for women's rights!

I had a child; she had a lover. But ours was a friendship between girls, between students, because I was alone and she was free. She seemed to hold the right to work and the right to love as birthrights, while in my world, and in my land, men reserved those privileges jealously to themselves; and she brought me the message of a less purely intellectual civilization besides. At that far latitude she had come down from I pictured the narrower earth tapering off into a spindle, an antenna. I glimpsed a light from Asia, too, softened through a veil of snow but still searing bright. And sometimes I wonder if it was not her almost flat cheekbones that first evoked for me the mystery of the hundreds of millions of Chinese.

When I saw Joseph again, on his first leave, I remember how different I thought him from the man I had described to Irina. His almost overrefined behavior, his faintly precious conversation, contrasted sharply with her great young freedom of manner and talk. On the other hand, my husband's antipathy for my friend was immediate, and it was never to be overcome. He found her conversation woolly-minded and her cheekbones Mongol. He was too intellectual not to mistrust anything irrational; he disapproved my having joined that esoteric society and resented Irina for having met me in such a place. In a sense, he was right not to like her; unintentionally, and even unwittingly, it was indeed she who turned me away from him. When I saw her in love with her magnificent Clarke I began to judge Joseph, to think him less a handsome boy, less a virile one, and to dispute his opinions.

It was then, too, that I wondered for the first time what had become of my cousin Augustin Costa, who had pleased me so when I was eighteen, and who had displeased my parents so by his ideas (even then)—ideas which I had come to hold myself without realizing that they were his. From Höberlin I could learn only that he had founded the French labor party

37

he had told me of on that long-ago night when we danced together.

In May of 1940 Irina left for England; she did not reappear in my life until 1944, married to her American and younger than ever, despite totally white hair at the age of twenty-five. She went with Clarke to America; then, after her divorce, she left for Canada alone. And I have seen her only twice since then.

But I always tell myself the story of her life when my own is sodden with monotony. Her Finnish fiancé, dead of cold, frozen to death between the lines; that handsome drug-addicted Clarke, whom she left when she saw herself on the point of succumbing to the temptation herself; then her liaison with the German orchestra conductor, whom she sees only rarely, and with difficulty.

I mused over it all—it was the only dream and adventure I would ever know.

But is this what Irina calls the rediscovery of the world? This mournful need that has grown into an obsession—to work in an office from nine till twelve, from two to six, and to earn a little more money than Madame Bouquet at the end of each month?

A woman used to be judged by the way she submitted to the ritual of mourning. Today she is admired for her rapidity in returning to the world. I wear light mourning, but I do not agree with everyone else that it makes no difference, and that it is only the "feeling inside that counts." On the contrary, I believe that there has been a general lowering of the "*tonus*," so to speak, of suffering; and that the dead disappear more quickly than they used to.

I think that a woman who loved someone passionately and exclusively would shroud herself in black to hide from others the body that he would never see again; I know that such a woman would never rouge her face again, the better to resemble her own future corpse; I know she would loathe life, and loathe herself for her very aliveness. The nineteenth-century's formalism knew exactly what it was doing when it imposed heavy and light mourning, black wool and then white crepe; it drowned widows in a uniform tide, so that the merry widow could not be told from the other. Today they are no more easily distinguished, but this is not solely due to the disappearance of a certain formalism. It is also because the sensitivity of all beings is less sharp. There have probably been too many deaths in the past twenty years—too many unjust deaths, too many bloody deaths, too many mass deaths; the survivors are saturated with death. Any single death has lost some of its sacred meaning. I think I should like to find a hiding place to die in, as a bird does.

So I went to dine at the Höberlins'. Joseph's memory may not be an immense flame inside me, but it is a night light that will never go out; or at least less quickly than a fire of passion. Yes, I realize more and more how much I owe to Joseph.

We no longer loved each other, Joseph, why not admit it to ourselves now? But love is not the only thing in the world. I was young, Jo; I still hoped for the love of another man! I dreamed nostalgically of that Augustin Costa I had hardly known. I forgot that I had loved you very much, too, and that love can sometimes be no more than a fleeting crystallization. You were the first to ask me to marry; those words had a magical power for me—I was bewitched more by them than by you. Someone once said "First love is not the indelible one; it comes from the need to love." That may be true. Yes, if Augustin had asked me to marry him, it is he I should have loved. I was so near to it, so taken with him the night of my first ball, but he did not ask me to marry him! In those days those were the only words an eighteen-year-old girl wanted to hear. (And suddenly it occurs to me that it might have been that hope—unconscious on my part then, but certainly clear to him—that put him to flight so swiftly the day after that night.)

The truth about a couple is what survives when love is gone. We still had our confidence, our security. We still had being a pair. I should have been happy with Joseph, simply because he existed. Simply because he was my man, among all the men on this earth, and the six hundred million Chinese I kept dinning into his ears. Oh, I was often bored with you! Well, I am more bored now. I used laughingly (or without laughing) to call you pompous, the heavy father, or the narrow-minded technician—I don't know what else. But for a scientist you had an unusual degree of literary cultivation, and when you recited to Jean-Christophe from *Ruy Blas*, whom you had played on the stage at the prison camp, I recognized something of the tall young man who had won me by quoting Péguy! Your opinions were reactionary, and I minded them more than anything else. But you died at fifty: what we call destiny, the dark instinct that guides us all, had warned you that you would not need to move into the future.

You have had your revenge, Joseph. When I arrived at the Höberlins', I understood. There was nothing but couples. I was alone in being alone. They had had to invite a man to fill the void that you left opposite me, Jo. A single man. This one had plucked eyebrows and polished nails. But I had only to hear his high, precious voice ... Annie had not gone to much trouble to find me a partner, and I resented it all the more because I know she never leaves anything to chance.

Annie, the wife of my old enemy Höberlin, is so completely opposite from me that I realized on the day they were married how unattractive I must be to Georges: as unattractive as he was to me! Too redheaded for my taste, too round, now the mother of six children, Annie is the kind of person I call the young matron: strong from her sixfold experience, sure of herself, always ready to issue a piece of advice or a doctor's address. Her eye, as round as herself, surveys her friends with the same glance her children get. Nothing escapes her: not the hastily patched-together conjugal quarrel, nor the liver ailment indicated by a yellowy eye, nor a white hair, nor the pale stain on the tablecloth that gives away the fact that it has been used before and carefully refolded. Annie has the infallibility of people who devote immense seriousness to very small things. When I used to entertain it was always Annie who would come involuntarily to mind; I would ask myself continuously what "the young matron" would think. This evening I knew only too well what she had thought. I could almost hear her saying to her husband the minister: "Whom shall I invite with Madame Fontaine? Widows and divorcées are very annoying; there are more of them than there are bachelors...." And Georges bursting into laughter: "The poet, of course! Costa's very literary!" For my partner was a poet. He drove me home in his car. They are always very nice to women.

But the Höberlin dinner did serve some purpose. I reminded Georges that he had promised to find me a job. There is one

41

good thing about an old enemy—one's relations with him are stripped of all complication, the dislike is undisguised, and the (rare) compliments more sincere than those of old friends. I consider Höberlin as intelligent, ambitious, and opportunistic as his face indicates him to be: thin lips, foxy nose. As far as he is concerned, I know he thinks me complicated, naïvely idealistic, sharp in appearance and nature; and when he looks at me I always feel ugly.

But we have known each other such a long time! I call him "old George," in English, and he stubbornly calls me Costa. I believe he respects my naïveté; he believes I admire his success. Within a day he found me what I had been seeking for a month. Suddenly, without knowing exactly how it happened, I was adorned with a magnificent title: General Secretary of the Four Cardinal Points Society; instructed to organize student travel and an exchange program for professors and for young foreign girls; and installed in a dark dirty office in the Latin Quarter. It is only a temporary position, but for three weeks now my evening dress has been hanging in the shop of a secondhand dealer; I took off the silk label that said *Marion Rapp*, and the dealer pinned on the depressing notice "For Sale."

I will always remember how the bundle of paper money I drew at the end of the first month had the fragrance of a loaf of bread, the weight of bullion in my hand. I was as proud and as tired as if I had scaled a mountain. But I held myself straight again, and I breathed deeply as I walked, as if I had bought the right to breathe as well.

I was able to send Jean-Christophe the long-playing Monteverdi records he wanted for his birthday; he will find them at

Toulon next time he comes into port. Choosing them, I felt a moment's happiness.

I have always sought out conversation with those characterized as the "common" people. I tried not to seem too much a maternalistic social worker, or to sound like Georges Höberlin saying, "How's it going, grandpa?" to all the old people in his constituency, and talking familiarly to the young ones. Nothing is harder for a member of the middle class than acting natural with the more humble. He may be a radical politician or a leftist intellectual, but he cannot avoid the tone of a benevolent society woman. Neither do I—I have no illusions about that. Especially I—I used to listen to the Italian bricklayer, the Moslem garageman, the Chinese manicurist, my little hairdresser, or Madame Bouquet, but I would do it as much to soothe my guilty conscience toward them as to hear what they had to say. Since I have gone to work I have lost the inferiority complex my social position gave me. I feel comforted to see that the young secretary who is the only other employee at the Society considers me her equal.

I call her Eliane, but I have not yet had the courage to tell her to call me Sylvestre. That rare first name, given me because I was born on Saint Sylvestre's Day, the thirty-first of December; that name that I used to dream of making famous when I was still Sylvestre Costa; that name that no man has ever pronounced as I would like to hear it—I want to keep it for myself alone a while longer. But we help each other, and an immediate fellowship has grown up between us. Simply because there hangs over us the elusive might of the international organization that finances the society, toward some purpose that we will never know exactly—which may be an altruistic one, but which in any case escapes us.

I have often tried to imagine what I would feel at working for someone else. Because, ultimately, one is always working for someone else. Of course one is paid, and in that sense one works for oneself. But the material one works with belongs to the other person; it slips between your fingers like the hidden object passed from hand to hand in the children's game—you give it a bit of your own warmth, and you never make back that expenditure. The saleswoman in a luxury shop, for example, into whose hands the owner or the factory messenger delivers the blue alligator bag, the antique alabaster lamp, the diamond clip; the blond-rinsed, dark-clad saleswoman who lives amid the shimmer of Lyon silk, of Baccarat crystal, of Chinese porcelain, or high-warp woolens, who holds the precious objects only to put them into other hands, without that endless glow's leaving a single trace on her own hands—unwittingly (though she does sense it obscurely) that woman is that most ambiguous thing in the world: the intermediary. Like the stenographer who writes words she does not understand to a man she does not know. And the accountant who manages fabulous sums of money. And the miner in the black glare of the coal, the mason who builds a house that is never his, the welder on the automobile assembly line. And I myself, who organize trips that I shall not take again.

It seems to me now that the object, the material, the work itself have such an importance that, fortunately, they mask the other fact from us. The essential thing is still the human warmth, slim as a gold leaf, that we manage to slip between the monotony of a daily task and the enormous machinery we are no more than a gear in. When my work grows tedious, I

44

recall the last film I saw with Joseph, *The Bridge Over the River Kwai,* and its hero, the British officer who identifies himself so completely with the bridge he had built for the Japanese that he forgets it was for the Japanese. And, of course, like him, I mourn my lost freedom. But what was I doing with it? When Colonel Nicholson looks back on the life he had led before his capture, he finds it negative, too.

Before, when I returned from a dinner with Joseph at one in the morning, I would try to imagine the thoughts of the North African night attendant who would watch us go by from behind his glass cage. In his eyes happiness probably had the shape of the big black limousine that drew into the garage and turned out its lights; and the form of the couple, also in black, who climbed back up the ramp on foot, answered his greeting, and disappeared toward the unimaginable comfort of a well-to-do apartment. If I had told him how impossible those dinners sometimes were, he would not have believed me. And he would have been right: that dinner bored me only because I had been to a thousand dinners like it. Oh, he should have been jealous for a very different reason instead—for the possibility of spiritual development, of perpetual enrichment that leisure gives. But what did I do with my leisure? What do the rich do with their leisure? And what would the poor do? Society is going to undergo a total upset—all right. There will be other people eating the good dinners, that's all it will mean. But behind the bars of a far larger cage than the night watchman's there stare the wide-open eyes of my six hundred million Chinese.

The office stays open during the lunch hour, and Eliane and I change off, so that we have no chance to talk. But each evening I walk down the Boulevard Saint-Michel with her. We

45

separate at the Boulevard Saint-Germain; she takes the 63 bus to the Gare de Lyon, then the train to Villeneuve Saint-Georges where she lives with her father, a former sailor turned gardener. I take the 63 in the opposite direction. When we are late, she is lost in those distracted little calculations that make up the shifting foundation of life in large cities: cross before the red light to get the half-past bus, and catch the train at quarter of. But when we have time we chat while we walk relaxed, and each time I marvel at her precise, modest intelligence.

She senses vaguely that I come from *elsewhere*, that I don't belong to her world, but she is too discreet to ask a question. When I tell her that I am a widow, she cries, "Oh! Now I understand," and I see quick shadows pass over her small shadowless face, one after another—first an immediate pity, then an understanding older than her years—and finally the bright shadow of a mysterious satisfaction wins out.

"I *knew* you must have had some trouble. I'm proud I guessed," she admits. "What did your husband do, Madame Fontaine?"

"He was an engineer."

She does not answer. Eliane never speaks when she does not know what to say. I go on: "What kind of boy would you like to marry?" She is twenty-four, and very frightened of becoming an old maid; she is not happy with her father, who drinks, she told me one day. She does not hesitate for an instant:

"I would like someone who's fond of me and who doesn't drink."

I felt the blow right in the heart. I had said "engineer." But for her she asks nothing—neither money nor a better social position, not even the kind of looks that attract her. . . . She is intelligent, she has a diploma, she is an executive secretary. And she speaks English! But all she asks is that her husband not drink. . . . For the past three years I have wondered what cause I could ever give myself to totally, and I decided very soon that there was none—not even Augustin Costa's labor party! Why not that one—except that I was convinced of the vanity of personal efforts? I have always been hypersensitive to the insignificance of the individual; I have always felt myself small as an ant.

Since I have gotten into the habit of receiving my monthly salary regularly I have an agreeable sense of security, and Madame Bouquet comes in again every morning. I have even ordered a small two-cylinder car, which I hope to have in the spring. But with each stair that is climbed, another presents itself to be scaled, and the new one becomes all-important to your eyes. When I come home tired, and find myself alone again in an empty apartment, I feel my life is an absurdity: I work to live, and my life is not really essential to anyone. Except to Mother, of course. But since she is a widow (she, too), she no longer belongs entirely to the world of the living; she has visited the cemetery every day for the past six years. Jean-Christophe loves me, but he loves Nadine more, fortunately. After next year he will go into the large export-import house his father-in-law runs in Marseilles. When I die he will inherit my Directoire furniture—why not do him that favor right now? What else can I hope for but this job, which saves me from asking help of my son or my mother, and after this, another job like it? I expect no surprise from life. A man? Oh, yes, it's true, there are men. There is even love. At least so they say. I think of the two Rapps, but they are twenty-nine, both of them. That is another generation than mine. I am one of those who were twenty years old before the war—another world. I knew that world where everything was absolute: religious faith, the nation, art, and love. Today everything is relative. (Even faith. "I believe, but . . . ," say the best Christians.)

When I refer so often to the Chinese, it is because I am obsessed by the thought that there are forty-five million Frenchmen, that Jean-Christophe and Nadine are part of the number, and that their children will grow up in a world where there will be a billion Chinese. That figure is a way of making my anguish concrete. Some people go into psychoanalysis, some are neurotically fearful in cars, others try not to think of anything at all, like the two Rapps, and to earn as much money as possible. When he senses how I am obsessed by war and cancer, death and afterlife, Jean-Christophe tells me, smiling, "Have faith in the future, Mother; you taught me that choosing for the future is the only decision that can't be wrong!" But unconsciously he has changed the meaning of the lesson I had tried to teach him: "Be aware of the future, it is the single irresistible force. Try to anticipate the future. . . ."

What can I do to save Jean-Christophe's future? It is really the only future I would live and die for, but what can be done? At another time I would have answered, "Politics." But everything has grown more obscure, almost occult. Everything seems to have rotted. I accused Joseph of being indifferent. I am not; I have never been capable of indifference; but I feel myself powerless. My father used to say, "If a person is neither a Communist nor a Christian, he is nothing at all." But he only said it after his conversion, in his older days. From that

48

time on I had moved toward a kind of detachment, very far from indifference, but which would have forbidden me to mix religion and politics. In fact, as time goes on I am more conscious of the abyss that separates the world from what is so aptly called the Other World. Oh, no—the kingdom of God is not of our world. Far from turning themselves into workers, priests should become hermits or preacher-monks again; they should station themselves under the crosses at intersections, to remind helmeted motorcyclists and motorized farmers, whether they want to hear it or not, that the present shape of the world is nothing but a momentary fluke in the cosmic evolution, that everything will return to dust—the dust of energy that will rise after the last atomic explosion, and spray this earth and those skies into infinity. Ah! We worry about many things. But an unnoticed seed, hidden deep in the eye of these whirling cells, awaits the moment of the most perfect chemical composition —the one which will finally annihilate the most by the least and will re-establish the primordial nothingness. And the earth and the sky will have passed, according to the Word, making way for the new creation.

When I used to speak of these things, Joseph would shrug his shoulders and smile. One day he told me, "Actually, you're a Manichean." And it is true to some extent. But why did he always smile, the few times when we spoke of our ideas? I would close up immediately, less wounded by his protective reaction than reassured by the oldest feminine reflex: the hope that one's learned husband knows more about it. As long as he was there, I felt safe from anguish. I hid myself in Joseph's knowledge, as the ostrich hides its head under its wing. But I was the one who was right, I know that now. There is no longer a screen between me and horror. Because I am alone, I

49

hear better the sound of the wormwood waters rising from the chasm. And I know that I shall die alone.

I was thinking of all this on my way to dinner with Paule du Haut-sur-Pas. In my fanlike array of friends she is the intellectual. When I felt myself growing stupid, I would get myself invited to Paule's; and each time I met someone who would send me home satisfied, my mind waked up.

Paule is a philosophy professor; but she has made a miniature studio out of the mansarded attic room she bought after saving for ten years, and she serves excellent dinners on her bridge table. I meant it when I told the incredulous Paule that her life was a success. It did not seem to me that for a woman as independent and as intelligent as Paule to do without a husband was an absolute tragedy. If I had dared, I would have mentioned the Amazons, who cut off their breasts to ensure their renunciation of love.

Arriving at her room, I found a sick young actor she had mentioned, livid in a black beard, but with the damp, touching gaze of a good dog. There was a former nun, still young, named Alexandrine, who, having had the misfortune to lose her faith, had been released from her vows by the Pope after ten years of struggle. And finally, two of Paule's students: a Rumanian refugee, and a young girl who wore red woolen stockings and a single braid wrapped around her head the way I always imagine Virginie. As heterogeneous a collection as in a railway compartment. We were so crowded that Paule set the platters in the center of the table, and we served ourselves from them.

I did not understand all of the conversation among the two philosophy students and the atheistic nun. To them, the absurd

—they talk of nothing else—is a bearable state, because it is that of the human condition par excellence. "If we refuse to accept the absurd, we might just as well give up life," said the young girl who reminded me of Virginie. They do not believe in literature any more, but in a kind of pathos (the word is mine), where time replaces man, and the object replaces the plot. They referred frequently to a special issue of some review, devoted to new literature, that I had not read.

I felt myself out of my element and incompetent, and at the same time happy to be there, glad to see young, intelligent people who did not seem to despair at living in our time, who believed in the future. An absurd future, but a future nonetheless. Whenever I hear a young person express his hope, I rejoice: I tell myself that he is thinking for Jean-Christophe and that Jean-Christophe is living for him. It may be selfish, but I am his mother.

"The moment you accept that nothing has meaning, everything takes on meaning," concluded the nun, laughing. "It's astonishing to see how the things fall into place again then. . . ."

Alexandrine talks too loud, she laughs nervously, and I watch her eat with a vague sense of sacrilege. She is beautiful. Twelve years of convent have kept her youth intact. I know from Paule that her family turned their backs on her, that men draw away from her as if she wore a cross tattooed on each cheek, and that she hesitates to accept the only work offered her—as an attendant in a women's prison. Oh, the mockery of it! I imagine her veiled, cloistered for over ten years performing actions grown meaningless to her. And now alone, crushed by a freedom hard to bear. In her terrified eyes I read a nostalgia —which she will never admit—for that enclosure where she would at least have died without feeling fear, as I would in Joseph's arms.

It is terrible, isn't it? I know how terrible it is, I wanted to tell her, as after dinner I watched her reapplying lipstick—too much lipstick—with scrupulous care. Lighting cigarettes one from another—endlessly. And the least of her gestures seemed indecent. Absurdly indecent.

Paule spoke little, busy serving her good dinner and watching over the bearded actor, whom she called her "pet." (His name is Léon.) I know people call each other "pet" in theater circles, but on Paule's professorial lips the word was as out of place as smut. The bearded boy did not talk either; his dog eyes followed her about. After dinner it was he who piled the dishes in the sink and spread a cloth over them. His moist skin, his unhealthy look hurt me—in our time we see few people so ill—and I often sought the eyes of the fresh girl that Virginie would have resembled in five years. But I always came back, despite myself, to the young nun; uneasily, because it seemed to me that her story was something like my own.

When everyone left, Paule signaled to me to stay. Then she let her single thought rise to her lips, and invade her unlovely face.

"What do you think of him?" she asked, anxiously.

"The little Rumanian?" I asked cruelly.

"No, Léon."

I look at Paule, and I tell myself once again that the love life of irreparably ugly women must be more curious than other people's, and that writers are lazy if they concern themselves exclusively with the problems of attractive women. (Perhaps in the new generation, thanks to the change of perspective predicted by those three young people—perhaps ugliness would

52

come into its own again? Like poverty in the last hundred years. For centuries no one was interested in anyone but ancient kings, or in all the princesses of Clèves. The soldier, the slave, the confidante—another class of intermediaries to life—were disposed about the stage without anyone's even suspecting that they, too, had a destiny. . . .) Awkward in her large body, Paule is one of those women who can burn their tongues brutally by putting the wrong end of a lighted cigarette in their mouths (she did it before my eyes), or sprain their ankles walking across their single room (that happened to Paule, too). Such women seem innately clumsy, when actually they are only discomfited by the burden of body and skin.

And yet, ten years ago, she did have a brief affair. I gaze at her yellow skin, her gray teeth, that enormous body; I imagine her shapeless bosom. How connect that image to an image of love? What do cruelly ugly women say to men before they show themselves naked? Do they hope that the nude truth of their bodies, that animal flesh, will wipe out the truth of their faces? Suddenly, intuitively, I visualize them wanton. . . .

"Sylvestre," Paule asked me, "what do you think of him?"

This time there was anguish in her voice; my silence panicked her. Her voice jerked me awake. But she had asked me one of those questions that should never be answered. The importance she attached to it proved to me that she herself had already answered the question; she only awaited approval. I hesitated.

"He looks very sick."

She swept the objection aside impatiently.

"Yes, unfortunately, they're going to operate again. Well?"

"He didn't say much." I felt my way carefully. "Your guests . . ."

She interrupted me. "Naturally, he had nothing to say, he's not an intellectual. Neither is he a . . . handsome man. But is that absolutely necessary?" she demanded aggressively.

"He's an actor, isn't he?" I asked with some effort. "Did he go to the Conservatory?"

"Everyone goes to the Conservatory," Paule replied with magnificent scorn. "That's exactly why he wouldn't!"

Till then she had been standing before me, her crossed arms supporting her overflowing bust, as if it were she and not I who was undergoing the interrogation. Suddenly she dropped into a seat beside me; her chest fell. I saw her plain face close up. But a very gentle, sad intelligence glowed in her eyes, the intelligence of a woman and not at all that of a philosopher; and her voice was slow and reasonable.

"I know very well," she said, "that everyone will say I'm wrong, because he is much younger than I, and because we will be living on my salary. But even if what everyone thinks is true—that I'm buying myself a man—what harm can there be in that?"

I was tired. The room smelled bad; it was too small for the six people who had eaten there. But I was spellbound by the melancholy of the world Paule was leading me into. All at once her voice hissed, "I'm forty-six years old, and I have no one in the world . . . I don't want to grow old alone in this maid's room—I don't want to! You know what I want? I want a child!" she finished, her tone provocative and yet adamant— the tone she must use when she enunciates some philosophic paradox to her students.

It was all so unexpected, so embarrassing in a way, that I had to fight down an abrupt urge to laugh uncontrollably. I fled to safer terrain.

54

"Where did you meet Léon?"

The brief challenge Paule had thrown out, and that I had not picked up, was enough to crumple her once again. An interminable silence. Her cat jumped up onto the bed between us. I detest animals, but the strange discomfort that lay motionless under the slanted ceiling was such that I had to find something to do and I stroked Néant. And suddenly there was that impersonal voice of a desperate woman, those obsessive eyes staring straight ahead, unseeing, while Néant slid under my hand and escaped as if I disgusted him.

"Léon is the son of Russian refugees. He has no more family either. He registered at an agency. . . . He simply asked for 'an affectionate woman, tall, of authentic nobility.' It's incredible, but true—No, don't look at me, Sylvestre! That was my agency. Yes, for several years now I've been on their list of women seeking gentlemen, 'of suitable age and position.' Well, I thought, for the first time in my life my aristocratic name might serve some purpose. You see, Léon is foreign: my name gives him a sense of oldness, of roots, of belonging. . . . Now kiss me and go away quietly, without answering me. I don't know why I've told you all this. . . . Still, there is one more thing I want to say before you go. You must certainly remember the story I told you ten years ago about the medical student. . . . Well, it wasn't true, Sylvestre. I invented everything but the boy's existence. Everything. Now you understand. I want to be a woman or die."

I ran down the service stairway. I had no more desire to laugh. I would have liked to leave Alexandrine's glance and Paule's voice behind me forever. But it was impossible. I had undergone another initiation, and, like all the others, this one was irrevocable. I had undergone a *reverse initiation*. I was back in the strange world one lives in when one knows no men —the boarding school, the convent, the sultanless harem, the prison camp, the insane asylum, the women's reserve, more secret than Indian reservations—the world of abortive desires, where men have the substance of shadows, where overweening loneliness creates phantoms more real than any true thing. The world I now belong to, whether I want it or not. But if neither the nun nor the philosophy professor could live in it, how could I ever manage to bear it? Impossible! I have a body, too. I had forgotten that.

Since I have become a widow, I am irresistibly attracted to the gray fringes of life, the edges of society, the places where there occur all the things we talk about in our own circle without living them—the men who drink up their wages, the women who haunt the marriage bureaus. One Sunday a short time after I dined at Paule's I had lunch at Villeneuve-Saint-Georges, with Eliane.

She looked delightful in her good dress, black and simple, and with her nails polished, an indulgence usually prohibited by her typewriter. She lives with her father—the former sailor —in a two-room apartment. The father occupies the bedroom, and Eliane has only a bed by the dining table; all that fineness, all that freshness has no other refuge but a couch in a corner of the living room. A few books, with not a best seller or a cheap novel among them; a few photos on the bed table—the only corner in the world where Eliane is entirely herself. Beyond the borders of that tiny corner the reign of universal ugliness begins. The classic ugliness of the three seascapes in deep leatherette frames: one black and one green—"Tempest" —one blue—"Fair Weather." The incomparable ugliness of the hanging model ship, like the ex-voto of little Breton ports: I can see electric bulbs behind the portholes. The gigantic ugliness of the long string curtains, boiled, boiled, and boiled again.

In the next room, almost as if I could hear it (but I do hear it, I do!) I sensed the heavy breathing of a dead-drunk man. I followed Eliane's glance, and I saw the blue, bloodshot eyes as he poured himself a shot of liquor: the gardener's fingers trembled so badly that he clutched his glass in both hands and felt for his mouth like a blind man. He is still young; the worst of it is that even in the midst of his disintegration he still has the hard beauty of a one-time sailor. When Eliane left the room for a moment he looked at me, at first out of the corner of his eye, slyly, then square in the face. In the streaked eyes I saw the glint of another kind of madness. I did not want to show I understood; I stared back into that gaze that grew steadily more fixed. And suddenly I saw my transfigured self in that wet stare, reflected as in a glass of wine: the red, damp image of a Sylvestre I had forgotten. For an instant of obscene complicity I—

I rose and joined Eliane in the kitchen. She was arranging hors-d'oeuvres of all colors on a platter. Her motions seemed as easy and graceful as an actress's in a commercial. She smelled of lavender. She looked like a cover girl for a women's magazine. Without looking up at me she said, "You saw, Madame Fontaine."

It was not a question; I was not expected to reply. She added, and her clear voice trembled, "He's in very good shape today. He knew you were supposed to come. But there are days—sometimes he frightens me. He loses all control over himself, you understand. . . . I lock my door every night."

She repeats, "You understand, Madame Fontaine?"

57

I understood, but there was nothing to say. I also understood the meaning of her words—"who loves me and who doesn't drink." I had been surprised that her ambitions stopped there. I was very naïve. There are hundreds of thousands of women who have seen only the worst aspects of men. How could they have any more than negative hopes?

Of course I had known that. But it is a very different thing to worry generally and altruistically, from the haven of the upper middle class, about the number of alcoholics in one's country, or to be kind to an unfortunate friend. (Not so long ago I considered that Paule owed me a certain gratitude simply because I would invite her to go to the theater with me when Joseph did not want to go out!) It is a very different thing to be the Madame Fontaine of a year ago and to be the one I am today. It was the present one that Paule confided in. It is to the present one that Eliane says sweetly, "I would like to be like you!" Reject its effects as I will, it does me no good to rebel against this undesirable sisterhood, nor against the new equality that exists among us.

How slim the barrier is now that separates me from Paule or from Eliane! A few years from now, will I sound like Paule when, swallowing all shame and forgetting all philosophy, she murmured, "I don't want to grow old alone in this room; I don't want that"? Already, in the office, Eliane and I sound alike. On the telephone people mistake us. It is a very frequent phenomenon, this kind of mimicry, I know; but I see a symbol in it.

All my previous pity was a luxury. Pity is a luxury. Charity is a luxury. The pity of the happy woman is an insult to the other. I know this, I who flee Marion's. "Someone who doesn't drink" . . . "Is it absolutely necessary for a man to be handsome?" … "They should train all women to be widows." People didn't say things like that to me *before*. How could I have suspected, caught as I was in the workings of my married life, accustomed to Joseph as to a comfortable coat, how could I suspect that a man like Joseph was a rare treasure? My God! How sheltered I was! I thought it completely a matter of course to be married to that man—a man who did not drink! Blind! Nothing is a matter of course, not even light. Everything is a gift. Even light, and a husband.

Since I am a widow—it is curious—the world seems populated solely with women, and the life of a single woman bristles with humiliating difficulties. I have sworn to win out over the ridiculous sensation that something is hostile to me, something that I cannot define; I am sure I will succeed. But meanwhile I find it hard to pay the tax that I did not expect, and just in December, when I wanted to buy a gift for Jean-Christophe. I find it frightening to have the grippe, all alone. Terrifying to come home alone at one in the morning, on the last Métro, and to be followed to the door by two silent North Africans—silent, but near enough for me to hear them breathe. And Mother's two suitcases are too large for the elevator, and I found them heavy to carry when she came to spend Christmas and Saint Sylvestre's Day with me.

Jean-Christophe had promised me he would come, but when he heard that his grandmother was coming up to Paris, he asked if he might spend his leave at Marseilles with Nadine: "Unless you're absolutely counting on me, Mother." I saw myself in the mirror, for the first time, a mother-in-law. And it was not pretty. But how could I tell him the truth? He thinks me brave; he admires me enough to tell his friends and Nadine herself, "My mother's a terrific woman."

Women, women, nothing but women. All day long Eliane's lavender scent. And Mother in the evening. I spent the two holiday eves alone with her. The night of the thirty-first of December I jumped when the doorbell rang late; I was afraid it was the dozen roses that Jo ordered from one year to the next, from the same florist, on the day when he paid his bill— he would celebrate my birthday, my saint's day, and the last day of the year all at once. But the florist must have read the obituary in the paper and the dead husband's flowers were dropped from the order list. It was the telegraph operator for his New Year's tip.

I found Mother changed since last summer. My misfortune has hurt her. In a few months she has become an old woman. I sense that it has cost her great effort to come to Paris, and that she dares not confess to me how much she misses Bastia. Insular to her finger tips, she relates the Corsican gossip, under the impression it amuses me. My whole childhood was nourished with her stories about the reputed relationship of the Costas to the Bonapartes. As out of place in Paris as Napoleon's mother, she brought with her the austere atmosphere of an old province, but of a province where gusts of the vendetta blew. When she told me that Augustin has just been appointed to a very important position in the United Nations, her black eyes flamed with anger. At first I imagined that Augustin's success hurt her because he belongs to a branch of the family which was never Bonapartist, and which has rivaled our branch for a hundred and fifty years; till now the balance leaned definitely to our side. Augustin's father was an unimportant government clerk, and his son's own political career has not been an absolute success. After three years in the Resistance, he failed in his attempt to set his famous labor party going again. I followed

60

his career from a distance. "We feel the same way about things now," I thought, "but it's too late." And a sword slipped through my heart, so swiftly that I felt no pain.

Now that he had been named to the U.N., the count is clearly in his favor, and that made me melancholy.

"Does he know you're a widow?" Mother asked anxiously. "Did you send them an announcement?"

"No, why? I don't even know their address."

From her relief I could see that she feels my mourning to be a humiliation—a little as though I had been deceived and deserted! Finally she asked me, gently, and a shade embarrassed, whether I plan to marry again—later, of course, much later!

I laughed. "Oh, no, once is enough!" and immediately I felt ashamed. It is strange: sometimes I feel the temptation to say something absurd, surprising, even shocking; to console myself for *something* I cannot express, even to myself. In any case, I managed to horrify Mother: she blushed for me. I tried to divert the conversation.

"You spoke of sending *them* an announcement, Mother. Augustin is married?"

My diversion was a failure: I was disagreeably surprised by that involuntary association of ideas. But Mother said, all her contempt returning, "Yes, of course. I don't remember now to whom, but I do know he's spent his life deceiving her; all those Costas are bad husbands. They say he's ruined her, too, with his party. . . ."

"If he could ruin her, that means she was rich to begin with."

"Yes," Mother said. "I remember now. She's a banker's daughter. And I hear she loves him so much that she forgives him everything."

61

I did not answer. I felt sadder than usual without knowing why.

My mother asked me to go with her to a meeting of the Christian Widows' Association she belongs to; she would like to found a chapter in Bastia. I came away horrified. I did not know there were so many widows!

The older ones made up the majority: from seventy to ninety-five years. With their massiveness, with the feathers on their hats, and the gold watch chains on their busts, they were a startling proclamation of revenge over the weak sex. There was one, a century-old hag, her chin entirely bearded with white hairs, who wore three wedding bands on her finger to show that she had killed three husbands under her. The widows of my age were the rarest. The younger ones—the saddest— were spoken of as the "Indochina widows," the "Algeria widows," as though they had lost a country along with their husbands. There was a terrible melancholy about their youthful mourning, because they, at least, had had their husbands taken from them by someone, by something; and yet no one admitted the responsibility for it, and their sacrifice had served no purpose.

I came out of there blind and deaf. I never saw men any more, I never heard men's voices. What could be done for all those women, for so many women, I wondered, short of rendering them blind and deaf, too, so that they should become their own absolutes?

"Oh, yes," Eliane said to me the next day in her clear voice with its answer to everything. "Didn't you know that there are four and a half million single women in France, counting the divorcées and the spinsters, of course?"

I quoted her Isaiah's words: "In that day seven women shall take hold of one man." But Eliane has a precise mind, and for her the Bible is a picture book.

"Oh, no," she said, laughing. "Only three, that's enough! In Germany it's much worse...."

Not very long ago I had some vague idea that unless she were as ugly as Paule, any normal woman had a man: a husband, a lover, or a dead man. Like Irina, who had all three. But it is not true. I thought that because I was married. It seems the statistics are clear on the point: there are a million and a half women too many in France. Plus three million women who live alone—some are divorced, some are unrecognized mistresses. (And some are women glad of their independence, but how many of those are there? How many Irinas are there in France, or in America?) All together, that makes a good four and a half million lone women. One lone woman out of every ten French citizens. Ten per cent of the population, worthless money, a little ashamed of the name.

When I took Mother to the Gare de Lyon; when I saw her sitting on the berth in the sleeping car, so tiny in her old-fashioned Persian-lamb coat that falls to her ankles, so old with the velvet violets on her toque—my heart gave way, because I was staying behind alone, and because everything was terrible. It seemed to me all at once that I had too much blood, that my veins were swelling, my head bursting.... Mother guessed what was happening and she was afraid I would have one of those outbursts that she dreaded when I was fifteen. Her eyes beseeched me, and I controlled myself; I smiled till the end. And it might well be an end, really. Because Mother is seventy-five years old, and she looked very frail to me this evening. When I kissed her, when I inhaled the brief dry odor of the

63

fur, I longed to inject her with a little of that youth, of that useless strength, that had just inflated my blood; but it is impossible. Mine are the too-full, hers the bloodless, veins. We cannot share anything.

I had the terrible premonition that I would never kiss her again. But I will not worry; premonitions are always wrong.

Fortunately, during the two weeks she spent in Paris I managed to conceal the fact that the Four Cardinal Points Society will close after the Easter vacation. I have three or four months ahead of me to find other work. This time I will look with more confidence. But I am sorry; I have grown attached to that office, to that work, and to Eliane. I shall miss my job much more than I want to admit.

I have begun to read the want ads again, and to telephone my friends. Georges Höberlin was, as always, the first to propose something. I would spend two and a half years in South America, handling public relations for a large contracting firm run by a Frenchman, Monsieur Cordobal. Apparently everything depends on this Cordobal, for whom Georges asked me for a photograph. "He can't pay for a five-hundred-thousand-franc trip for a woman whose face he may not like," he told me. Then he pointed out that it is the only chance I would have finally to use the Spanish I know—"What a crazy idea not to know English," he concluded, just as he has each time we have seen each other for the past twenty-five years.

At first the proposition seemed tempting. Then I reflected. Thirty months without seeing Jean-Christophe? Thirty months all alone abroad? I postponed my answer. Fortunately, I do not have to decide before September; the construction does not begin until November—with what is springtime down there. But I did give Höberlin a picture of myself, anyway, for Monsieur Cordobal.

"Do you speak English?" The phrase may become a leit-motif in my life. It is the ritual question, now that I have been looking for work. I grow more anxious as time slips by. April, March, February—I count the months backward, glad to redis-cover that the deadline is still far away. I even do my accounts backward, sometimes, when I am short of money. I set down the amounts that I manage not to spend and I add them up. I reach some reassuring sums, but they are negative ones, and my ruse is futile. The other total, the real one, the one I avoid setting down, always exceeds the first. We don't know what it is to lack money until we have rejoiced that there is a month with only twenty-eight days.

Counting the months off backward is another lie. The earth turns, and as long as it turns, time goes by. February, March, April. Eliane will slip a cover over the typewriter. I will give the keys back to the concierge. Even now the Society is flying on a single wing; I will never know why it lasted for two years. Eliane was there when it was established and she knows no more than I do. Now and again prospective tenants come in to look over the premises; it is no longer my home. It is as though this episode of my life has not happened. Time runs on faster and faster. I have enrolled at the Berlitz School, and every other day at seven o'clock I go to take an English lesson.

Again I have asked Madame Bouquet to come only once a week.

I feel more and more regret at leaving this office where my working days are numbered, and even this work that I once found unpleasant. I love this tan-walled room and this desk with its purple inkstains. I was not wrong: the thing one imbues with a little warmth takes on human life. I cleaned the telephone myself each morning. I noticed that no one—not even Madame Bouquet, not even Eliane—knows how to clean a telephone. It is a world as complicated as an ear, and as I dig into the mouthpiece, as I turn its dial, as I stroke its wires, I feel the same sensual satisfaction that I felt long ago in washing out Jean-Christophe's ears, with the sense of unrolling their scroll work. But the telephone's are not the only secrets I know. I am the only one who can find my way through the apparent disorder of my drawers. He who can read the lines of a certain disorder would understand all about its creator. Two people can have the same order, but never the same disorder.

Eliane has already found a job as a cashier in a small hotel near the Gare de Lyon. She will begin in May, and I can see that she will not miss the Society; I believe she was bored here because our clientele is solely female! But for me the Society will always be the first place I worked, and all initiations have an absolute value.

Paule came in to recommend one of her students who wants to go to work in Ireland in exchange for board and room; it was she who unwittingly revealed to me how completely I had assimilated my role. When she arrived, I did not see her immediately. She heard me say to Eliane, "The Australians have rheumatism, but the Namur girl wants Druids." Laughing, Paule asked me to translate the code. It was indeed a code. My words meant that the Belgian-student-who-is-writing-her-thesis-on-the-Druids-might-possibly-agree-to-go-to-the-family-at-Ploumanach-where-two-elderly-Australian-teachers-refuse-to-go-knowing-that-the-Breton-climate-is-damp.

That day Paule told me that the former nun was dead.

66

I felt not surprise but consternation. Everything indicates that she killed herself with a massive dose of tranquillizers. It seems to me that I could have helped her, that I should have spoken to her. But could I have? What could have been said to her? Or done for her? She lived so forgotten in her rooming house that she was not discovered until twenty-four hours after her death, elaborately made up and wearing a short nightgown of a morbid, brazen richness.

Paule disappointed me: she spoke of Alexandrine without emotion, and she spoke of her in the past tense, as one speaks of people long dead. But Paule will soon be married. I felt that she already belonged to the other side—and that I no longer did. "Naturally," she said with a slightly superior tone, "Alexandrine did not make a completely free choice; she simply transferred her feelings. She came out of the convent to get married; that's quite a different thing from acquiring freedom." What jargon! Where is the trembling woman who one night unveiled the anguish of a person buried alive?

She probably still regrets her recent confessions. Her ugliness has taken on a kind of power. She no longer twists her ankles, she smokes casually, and she wears an engagement ring which would look real if it weren't so beautiful: an enormous brilliant set on fine gilded feet which Léon bought for a thousand francs in the Swiss Village. She bursts into laughter as she tells me this, she shows her thirty-two yellow teeth; she is bursting with laughter and with pride as well.

Perhaps she has already forgotten. But I shall not forget. I shall never forget again. Alexandrine is dead. Dead all alone. "I want to be a woman or die," Paule had said. Alexandrine was dead. I could not help telling her story to Eliane, but I made a mistake; I saw her small face disintegrate with panic.

67

"No one can live alone, Madame Fontaine, you see, you can't!" she told me, in the voice she has sometimes—ageless, full of some inherited experience, some old, old experience.

"Oh, yes," I said. "It's hard, but it can be done. I'm alone, too."

Her cry sprang from the heart, as they say—"But it's not at all the same thing, Madame Fontaine! You've lived your life!"

Cruel words: I had not known she considered me a finished woman. But she is right. A conjugal life, even an unhappy one, is still a life. Solitude, a life alone, is a kind of abortion, lived in slow motion. . . . And then I have Jean-Christophe, my power and my glory. Eliane has only her father. The night before he had vomited in the kitchen.

No, I will not forget. Paule has the right to forget: it is certainly her turn to live. But it is just as surely my turn to know. I know exactly the value of the happiness I had. But I was not, in the full sense of the word, a happy woman. Happiness excuses everything and needs no excuse itself. I was, above all, a member of the privileged classes—a privileged woman enjoying her material and conjugal security without remorse. Fundamentally, I was what I did not want to be.

Everything was taken away from me at once, and I succeeded to the difficult condition of a single woman. Let it at least teach me to become an adult responsible for myself. I am a lone woman: I shall accept all the consequences, I shall learn all its lessons, I shall suck the last drop and the bitterest. A widow like Madame Bouquet, a widow like Mother, alone as Paule or Alexandrine were. More alone than Eliane.

I recognize it with humility: before, I had understood nothing. I am appalled by that obvious truth: that one can understand nothing one has not first felt oneself. Nor is there any

68

love but the total identification with another, and if God made Himself man, this was the reason why.

But we cannot experience all forms of suffering; how many lives would we need to exhaust them all? An almost infinite number, say the Buddhists. Thus it is well that each new pain allows us to discover a new form of the universal pain. But pain is not a good in itself. To say so is a lie. To suffer is horrible. Suffering is evil. It is not an "enrichment," a "virtue." It is a stair to be trod, a rung to climb—not to wait there, but to discover another horizon. What I have discovered since I am a widow is boundless.

Like Moby Dick, the white whale—such is a man in the life of women. No, not only man. Just as the sailors of *Moby Dick* disdain the ordinary whales, and want to pursue none but the inaccessible, the fabulous, the fatal white whale, so do women pursue that great fish that is rarer than man: the husband. They go with vigilant eye, their chests heaving, and one night they crumple—as Paule did on that night already long past— they crumple half-dead, like gulls battered on the bridge of chance.

Why should my remorse about Joseph have grown less since I have known hunger?

I felt hunger only one night, it is true, and I knew I would eat the next day, but still, I knew hunger. Last week I was determined to finish out the month without drawing from the bank where I make regular savings deposits. The evening of the twenty-fifth there was nothing left in my billfold, and, through a ridiculous coincidence of circumstances, nothing in the refrigerator. I left the apartment at dinnertime, and, instead of buying bread, I surrendered to the temptation to buy

69

my weekly, the one that Joseph called progressive. As I paid the newsdealer, I saw that I was giving her my last coin. Pride kept me from retracting it and handing her back the paper. Besides, I wanted my weekly. And then again, perhaps—yes, I realize, I wanted to go hungry.

But when I passed by the ventilators at the bakery, the warm, tender, homelike fragrance rising from the ovens made me giddy. I went back to the apartment, and my hunger grew worse and worse. I settled myself on the couch with my paper, a glass of red wine, and a pack of Gauloises. I smoked the whole pack, I drank more than one glass of wine, and I did not read the paper. At midnight my hunger was atrocious. I had swallowed nothing since my sandwich at noon. First, hunger is an odor in the mouth. Then it is an ache. I tried to imagine how that odor and that ache could reach the fatal point. I slept heavily. The next morning, when Madame Bouquet brought fresh bread up with her, I was no longer hungry, but I had painful memories of the evening before.

Since that day, whenever I think remorsefully that I did not make my husband happy, I tell myself that if he knew that his wife, Madame Joseph Fontaine, had gone hungry, he would forgive me everything. And perhaps the whole business is absurd: if I had died first, he is the one who would have felt remorse. And if I died now, I am sure that Jean-Christophe would feel it, at the thought that he did not come to see me last New Year's Eve. Since his father's death he has spent with me only the six weeks that followed. He has never come again. If he has a pass, or two days' leave, they are for Nadine, and how can I reproach him for that?

When the conversation turns to children snubbing their parents or a family splintered by quarrels, how many times have I heard it said, "They're asking for eternal remorse! They'll see when he's gone. . . ." Alas, it is just another pious lie.

Yes, after the death of someone close it is intolerable to remember what one did to him, what one said to him; to wear oneself out going over some obsessing moment, longing to live it again some entirely different way. Then, later, his life takes on some distance, it congeals into its definitive form, and bizarrely, weirdly, everything about it comes to seem necessary.

I copied these words from Ecclesiasticus and put them prominently among my papers, so that Jean-Christophe would find them in case of my death. I love their secret humor:

"Weep bitterly, and make great moan, and use lamentation, as he is worthy, and that a day or two, lest thou be evil spoken of: and then comfort thyself for thy heaviness!"

I leaned hard on the final exclamation point, so that the boy should understand the sharp irony; so that once again, his tears already dried, he should say, "Mother is terrific!"

I am not at all terrific. I was silly enough to write Irina that I had "known hunger." She answers, and I seem to hear her laughing through the lines: "Let's say you were dieting, darling. . . . It's not pleasant but it's very healthy. Excellent for the complexion. You write that you thought of the Chinese, and that you were proud to be like everyone else at last. But you cannot have been hungry, because you were proud. When a person is truly hungry, he is ashamed."

I had a mass said for the first anniversary of Joseph's death. Jean-Christophe came to it. Forty-eight hours only, but he came. At last!

As I looked at him, I, his mother, should have liked to kneel before him. I found him taller, handsomer in his uniform, and I thought it miraculous to have given birth to this king, to this god that a son is to his mother.... What was I complaining of? What could I ever complain of? Jean-Christophe exists, and Jean-Christophe is happy. Just to hear him pronounce Nadine's name is to understand that he loves her totally and tranquilly. He loves her unpainted face—a pure face, betrayed by the sensual curl of the lips—he loves her body, perfect and unmysterious. (Mysterious no longer—I understood that without his having to tell me.)

I listen to my son, I gaze at him. I literally eat him with my eyes. Yes, I nourish myself on him. What amazes me most is his youth, not his manliness. I had forgotten that a person still looks like a child at twenty-one and a half. A man-child exactly. A man for Nadine, a child for me. How beautifully balanced life is, giving maturing women sons who are at the same time men and still their children! As each time I see Jean-Christophe I am aware again of the harmony of life, of the perfect curve it describes.

What strikes me in him is the facility he shows for being happy—his confidence in others, in life and in himself. It is our generation, my generation, that was complicated, troubled, and afraid. This one is simpler, and I would die sooner than bring my son into the tragedy of my complexities! Face to face with him, despite what he says, I feel antediluvian. (This is my term for everyone who was twenty years old before the last war.) I let him talk, endlessly. I watch him, insatiably. There is nothing more beautiful than a happy adolescent. I have always thought that the possibility of happiness is one of the proofs of the existence of God; contrary to most people,

I grow close to God when I am happy, and I find it very difficult to do so when I am suffering. What they call the "shame of the Cross" has always seemed to me the worst obstacle to faith. But now it appears, after some recent discoveries, that that cross of which it is written "Bear it to follow me," may simply be the distinctive mark the pious Jews wore on their foreheads in Christ's time—a tangible sign of their belonging to God and not a symbol of the required suffering. If this theory is verified, what an upheaval it would cause in our old Jansenist masochism! What joy never to have to carry a cross again, but to wear a star on our foreheads instead!

I wanted to give my son back his room. I arranged his bed and his belongings, and he felt immediately at home again. I had put a new LP and a photo of Nadine on his table. He said, "You're sensational! You worked all day long at the office and you haven't forgotten a thing!"

As I kissed him, I was thinking that he would sleep in my house only two nights, and that Nadine would have the right to breathe that odor for the rest of her life—that odor in which, inhaling it, I alone still recognize the stubborn, exquisite trace of his baby smell. She would have the right to stroke that hair, thick at the neck like a dog's; the right to listen to that voice, which for me, too, is the world's voice, singing counterpoint to records that I will continue to choose for him. I have resolved that, each time I am jealous of Nadine, I will rejoice, because it will be the sign that I feel Jean-Christophe to be perfectly happy! The day he needed me would be a terrible day. Very good, very good, this turning things upside down. A star on your forehead, Sylvestre!

I have finally moved back into my old room and the double

73

bed. I had thought I could never do it. And there—it is done. (There was also a day when I was able to look at Virginie's picture. . . .)

One year. . . . They say a year is a short time—but then, they say a great many things. Perhaps it is short, I don't know. It seems to me that it is life that deserves to be called short (and even then!): fifty or one hundred years. Then a year is very important: we haven't many of them to live. What merchant, with fifty precious stones in his possession, would not hold on to each of them as to his own eye? To me, the year that just passed has been interminable. It weighs more than all the rest of my life. Its heaviness crushes me; I cannot tell if it is of lead, or of gold, or bones; perhaps it is Joseph's astral body, or his soul escaped from some purgatory and come to visit me from time to time. I do not feel light, I have never felt light since his death. This year has the weight of a lifetime.

I mused a long while before that altar, sitting once again all in black beside Jean-Christophe in uniform. The Fontaine family was behind us; they knelt and rose rhythmically. It was Jean-Christophe who asked me to invite them to that mass: "You're above their meanness, Mother." Yes, my darling; I am above everything, I am terrific. . . .

Despite those eyes that I feel drilling into my back, I manage to pray. But in my own fashion. Without a word, without a formula.

I am no longer a practicing Catholic. I have never felt the presence of God, I have never known any kind of mystical certainty. After my father's death, at the end of his edifying old age, I never got the faintest answer when I implored him to show me some proof of his survival. Despite my negative experience at the "Cosmic Philosophy center" during the war,

74

I then joined a Christian occult society to try to make contact with my father's spirit: but in vain! Nevertheless, far down in me, and hidden like a flaw, there is a hopeless aspiration toward a state that must be called contemplative.

I never kneel. It seems to me that that uncomfortable position cripples the spring of a straight body, erect as an antennae. On my feet, my eyes closed, I make an emptiness in myself: first, I separate myself from the outside world, then I empty myself of myself; finally I concentrate my powers. This is no empty formula: athletes do the same thing when they concentrate in silence before their test. I feel as though I were calling forth the fluids that I usually let flow away, as though I were stemming a veritable hemorrhage of nervous power, and gradually I feel those fluids, those powers, draw together again around a central point that I do not try to identify. At such moments my breathing slows to such a point that once or twice I have imagined I was going to die. And I remain thus immobile, at once outside myself and returned into myself. Each time I open my eyes after my nameless prayer I feel as calmed, as renewed as after a night of sleep, or a long bath in tepid water. Perhaps it is only because I have managed to attain a certain degree of internal repose? The only person to whom I once dared describe this strange experience was, of course, Jo. He answered: "It's just another form of relaxation," and that very simple explanation reassured me. Or perhaps I did not want to look any further. . . .

I did not relax for long, in any case, before the altar where his memorial mass was being celebrated. It is easy to suffer at someone's death; it is easy to pray for someone dead. But where is *he?* What is he feeling? What unimaginable metamorphoses is he undergoing? That is what counts, that is what

75

is terrifying. What frivolity there is in the agnostic's words, "His suffering is over!" and what lack of curiosity in the believer's: "Now he is in heaven!" I always want to answer them, "Go see for yourself!"

And we'll all go see for ourselves whether we want to or not, won't we? Why are we not more curious about what we shall see then? Quite suddenly I remember reading a very simple and very profound sentence in René Bazin: *"We are dead longer than we are alive."* Words that would frighten you, if you decided to think about them.

When I was young and pious, I had a very simple idea of the beyond, based only on the hope that total Truth would finally be revealed. I was vaguely aware since childhood of the fact that all our truths are partial; then Irina, who was much further developed than I, encouraged me in that direction—I hoped to discover at the very instant of my death all the facets at once of the one Truth, of that crystal chunk that I should finally have penetrated to the center. We used to amuse ourselves, Irina and I, at imagining what might happen, in God's great joke. We liked to describe the surprise the saints must have felt on discovering that their bodies were not at all the accursed flesh, the instrument of sin that they had believed. So they always felt guilty? We roared with laughter—it was because they were! They had sinned by making their flesh an all-powerful force, in trembling before it, like Rosa of Lima who fed herself on five lemon seeds a day. We imagined the surprise of the saints: the opposite, for example, of Christian spouses'. These latter would discover that their sanctified gestures of love had nonetheless been a concession to the flesh, thus to the most perishable part of their beings. We replaced the idea of "sin of the flesh" by the idea of "the flesh-as-obstacle-to-transcendence," and we decided that the saints, the good Christians, and those who are called sinners come up against exactly the same obstacle—their bodies: the first by denying them, the second by tolerating them, the last by deifying them. We imagined a great exchange of excuses among them, a torrent of politenesses, till all the differences are abolished in a newly rediscovered unity. We married Casanova to Santa Rosa of Lima; then, satisfied, we came back down to earth.

I was so young, and Irina younger still! Newly healed of her dead fiancé, she had the exuberance of life that is characteristic of convalescents. But since then I have seen my baby, then my father, then my husband die. I do not think I have lost faith; but I have lost, one after the other, all the bright clarities of faith. Only the dark obscurities remain to me. To be sure, this year I caught myself wondering what truth Joseph has discovered—he who said constantly that when a person is lucky enough to have faith he has no right to question it . . . (I have no idea what I will discover myself; we do not know what we are.) And recently, when Alexandrine died, I hoped wildly that the little atheist nun had gotten the marvelous surprise of not being surprised, because at the cost of her life she had penetrated the secret of two contradictory and thus complementary truths, and that may be God's secret. But how anthropomorphic and how childish all of that seems to me in the face of this great emptiness that Joseph has become!

I envision God as so far transcending all that we can imagine of Him that it seems to me impossible that death—that liberation of a few particles of superior energy—is enough to return us to Him all at one blow. In our march toward God, death is an advanced stage, but it may not be the last. Theologians have concerned themselves very little with the problems of the beyond; but mystics, spiritualists, Hindus, who have pressed their research on the death phenomenon so far—they speak of a slow purification, an endless climb, a very difficult development toward staggeringly distant spheres. Oh! how frightened I am of God for Joseph and for myself—while the ritual unfolds and the Fontaine family sits and rises mechanically in a solid body. All those who have approached the mystery of God have felt Him to be a light surpassing even the idea of fire.

A year ago Joseph was a human being, my likeness, my twin. How did he react, confronted with the Fire? What did he become? A spark from the brazier? An angel? A star? A simple cluster of the universal energy? In any case, he has drawn dizzyingly far from me; beyond the farthest galaxies, beyond the farthest stretch of my mind. . . .

I remember that for opposite reasons he found Father Teilhard de Chardin and Simone Weil each as dangerous as the other. (We had read them at the same time.) I can still hear him telling me: "These are the kinds of theory that can only trouble you." Perhaps. What I did retain of them, in fact, is the rediscovery of our terrible distance from God—in time, for Father Teilhard, and in space for Simone Weil, who said that in relation to God we stand at the farthest point from which it is not totally impossible for us to return to Him.

Thus the only prayer I accept—and I repeat it once again while the priest gives the absolution and while the Fontaines move about behind me, impatient at seeing that again I have not wept—thus my sole prayer is David's prayer: "My God, why hast thou forsaken me?" Because it is less a prayer than a plaint, almost the hopeless acknowledgment of a fact. The very prayer of dereliction itself. And a crucifying doubt shoots through me: if Christ himself chose it from among all the prayers, He who knew by heart the Law, the Psalms, and the Prophets, perhaps it is because He knew better than we how forsaken we truly are.

Springtime awoke late, but abruptly, the day Jean-Christophe left. And everything around me began to burst into bud, as it does after a long winter.

To go to the station with Jean-Christophe, I take out my royal-blue coat; it is warm out, and I was sweltering in my black woolen things. Its blue heightens my coloring, makes me pretty. "How young you look!" Jean-Christophe exclaims, and I laugh: "That's because I wasn't very old when you were born!"

We laugh again as we embrace. I feel this leavetaking does not pain him: Nadine waits at the end of the journey.... Faithful to my pledge, I rejoice.

The Society office should be closed by now—we go in only to finish up the last details. I have already taken thirty English lessons; I am proud of understanding the BBC news on the radio. I shall be able to meet my next employer with the sacramental proclamation: "I know some English." For the moment I have no particular employment in sight. If necessary, I can wait till November. Why not leave then for South America, as Höberlin has proposed? Of course, public relations for Cordobal is not the United Nations! But why not admit it to myself—I feel a craving to move about, to travel, to live. At times my own body feels like a fruit. It seems to me that I could feed off its scent, live and die by that luscious ripeness that I am kept from sharing.

I expect my little car soon; I am taking driving lessons as well as my English lessons. I plan to start playing tennis again, too.

Eliane is not going to work as a cashier in the little hotel near the Gare de Lyon. She has become engaged to a pharmacy student from Villeneuve-Saint-Georges. She is happy and I feel as though I am marrying off a niece. Other people's happiness is a nice thing. Paule du Haut-sur-Pas has become Madame Léon Petroff, and I saw the expression of perfect happiness that should mark all young brides. I saw it in the Russian church on the Rue Daru, on the square face of the ugliest woman in the world, aged forty-seven, wearing a garnet suit and a white velvet hat! Oh, yes, other people's happiness is better than we think.

And then Martin Champell, on his way through Paris, does me good by forcing me to go out.

He is a friend of Joseph's, a bachelor, working for the Sahara Oil Company for the past two years. Martin is one of those men I call the chronic lovesick, whom every woman trails behind her, and who relapse into their illness at any kind word from her in a weak moment. I am fond of Martin, in the way I imagine I would have loved the brother I never had.

Martin telephoned me from the airport, and came to get me that same evening at eight. He is small and too fat. Actually I must confess that I find him quite ugly. But two years in the desert have ripened him; there is authority in his voice. Unfortunately, he talks as always about a single subject. It used to be ball bearings, now it is oil. Portia's line about one of her suitors, in *The Merchant of Venice*, comes to me each time I see Martin: "That's a colt indeed, for he doth nothing but talk of his horse."

He took me to dine at the Crillon, where he was staying. And he talks on about his horse Oil. Oil in time and in space; oil, from the well to the refinery; oil as a means of political pressure and of national wealth, oil in its derivative form of gasoline: the price of gasoline in Africa, benefits to the state thanks to gasoline.

Drunk as I am on oil, I am happy to be there. After all, it is oil that allows him to put me into his Citroën D.S. 19, and to open the Crillon doors to my dazzled eyes. The small glow at the end of our king-size cigarettes is oil. The authority in his voice, the assurance in his gestures—they come from the oil fumes rising to his head. And oil turns, bubbling, into champagne in our glasses. I had forgotten what a little money can do. I feel quite intimidated, as surprised and shaky as though I were just recovering from an illness. I am discovering that injustice which suddenly seems to me the worst of all: that a few paper bills can grant the right to beauty, while it is refused to Eliane, for example. I fix my mind for a few seconds on Eliane's crocheted curtains, and on her obscene buffet. Then I abandon myself to the pleasure of recognizing beauty, like a friend. Beauty—the glory of the silver service, the red roses that bloom on the tables like so many hearts. Beauty—the foreign couple dining beside us, bare shoulders and white dinner jacket, a pair so perfect that I cannot take my eyes off them. Are they real? Does such a man exist, his carriage like a god's; does such a woman exist, and that perfection in the harmony of her violet eyes, her flesh-toned shoulders, her dress with its three layers of chiffon bright pink, mauve, and soft green? Yes, they speak (in Greek, I think), they eat, they are living, like Martin and like me. Beauty—when we leave, the rustling stars of the Concorde and the Champs-Élysées; beauty—that

81

golden cabaret where Martin takes me, and where I hear and see from a few yards away the balladeer I listen to whenever he sings on the radio. I love songs to such a point that if I had been given some creative talent I think I would have liked, even better than writing a good book, to write some of those popular ballads which last no longer than one season, because they have caught the fleeting current and then died with it like fruits.

But how different it is to see this singer, here, in a dinner jacket with a flower in his buttonhole. When I listened to him at home I loved to hear him sing harshly of the cemeteries on the outskirts of Paris, of the black poetry of trampled lives. I would feel myself bound to the world's misery, and less alone. But in this setting I feel that the world's misery is betrayed— as when a communist deputy is caught in an American car. I am afraid of seeing into the tactics; I no longer recognize my Villon. Martin says: "This is the real Paris—it's charming!"

No. When I heard him, at my radio with my tray on my knees—noodles, ham, yoghurt—it was not charming, Martin, it was painful. Oh, no, Martin is not a brother. . . . If he were really my brother, I could say to him, "You are an ass, Martin! These songs are not at all charming, they are beautiful. They smell of poverty and absinthe, of wine and death, like Villon and Verlaine. You're an ass, Martin, if you don't understand that."

"A bit vulgar," Martin adds, looking at me apologetically, as if I were a princess he had brought to a low dive.

Personally, I think that here my balladeer has lost contact with his people. I loathe to hear about workers in a setting where no worker has ever set foot. But I am feeling too happy in the champagne euphoria and I have no desire to spoil my contentment. I smile like a coward and repeat the stupid words: "No, it's not vulgar. Yes, it's charming. Very Parisian, isn't it?" (Parisian!) I reach home all transformed, mad with beauty. Thank you, Martin, thank you, good night. Oh, yes, Martin, ask me again!

I have grown accustomed again to going out, with Martin Champell.

I used to be astonished that poor people found pleasure in reading tales of the gilded adventures of stars, princes, and billionaires—that old people in rest homes, sick people in sanatoria, could find amusement in watching the inaccessible lady announcers on television, or the gods of the sport world, or celebrated and surfeited men. I was wrong. We all need to believe that our unhappiness is exceptional, and that the luck of other people does exist: if everyone were sick, poor, and senile, then we would have reason to despair. But that health, that youth, that beauty seem to us the promise of a redemption on earth which is possible for us, too. In the starry windows of jewelry shops our poor-man dreams find flesh; they materialize and send their rays back to us. From being deprived of the superfluous, I shall at least have learned one thing: that the superfluous is not the useless; its existence helps to preserve the notion of beauty for those who are obsessed by the notion of utility. There are a few moments, at the heart of the bloody social injustice, when a mysterious, furtive balance is struck, when a kind of just vengeance occurs and when the roles are reversed: they are those moments when the poor man manages to enjoy pure beauty—without knowledge of its money value, without any idea of possession or even of desire, while the rich man must pay a price for beauty that prostitutes it.

Martin behaves with such obstinate protocol toward me that

83

I sometimes want to shake him by the lapels of his coat, to hit him on that large stomach (these strange desires have swept over me for some time now, to do something incongruous, to say outrageous words—what do they mean?). But that is not the Sylvestre he loves. He loves the stereotyped Madame Fontaine in my large wedding portrait—the one of the day he met me: black and white, the brown curls and skin emphasizing the symbol of the veil and the dress, as immaculate as a novice's habit; and those startled eyes that seem to be asking forgiveness for some mysterious fault.

Martin still bores me a little, and oil bores me a great deal. He has a good-scout side, too, which aggravates me, and when he speaks of his "little fellows from the *bled*" I could scream. But he is sweet, when he is not talking oil, the desert, or duty. He has a hobby: ethnography. It's a little austere, but it is a change. In any case I find it pleasant to have a friend to drive me to Fontainebleau, or to Rambouillet. Why should I refuse such innocent pleasures? I plunge into forests as other people plunge into water. I swim in a sea of ferns under a sky of Norway pines. Perhaps I found happiness in some forest in a previous life. I gather ferns by the armful, calling aloud to the druid priestesses as I go. For a day or two my apartment becomes a forest, I walk in lanes of ferns, in Merlin's enchantment. Every Saturday Martin takes me to the theater, or to a film. Then we have supper, and he begins once again to talk about oil. Occasionally I feel as though I am cheating him by being nice to him. But I am a little cowardly, like all women who are not yet truly accustomed to being alone. Perhaps I have also grown simpler. A man's friendship is good after this long fast. And so is the thought—quite curious and quite alone, like the first sprout in a wintry garden—that I could marry again if I wished.

Moby Dick.

For the first time I receive a letter from Irina in which there is the shadow of disquiet, in which her optimism quakes imperceptibly.

"I have just resigned from the Company, Sylvestre. Understand me: I resigned so that I should not be asked to leave. When I started with them, I had already passed the age at which stewardesses are normally dismissed. But you know what worked in my favor. Now it's over. They have accepted my resignation and they have given me a very important position—but on the ground. And then I shall not be seeing Wieland this year; he has just accepted an appointment that will keep him permanently in Munich, after having sworn to me he never would. His wife thus will always be with him. And I do not know how or when we will meet again. Write me quickly, and if you can, invite me to stay with you. I want to go to Europe this summer. Can I spend a few days with you, during my vacation? I need to know that a house is waiting for me somewhere in the world. . . ."

I sent her a telegram that same evening: "Come when you can. But stay Irina." I was disturbed.

If Irina's example deserts me, what will I become? Since I have known her, she has never confessed to a single fear or weakness. Her love for this German orchestra conductor, whom I have never seen, is the most beautiful I have ever known through living confidences; all the others I have lived through the dead pages of books. But Irina really had that encounter with Wieland in a plane ten years ago. Perhaps be-

85

cause it exploded five thousand yards above the earth, that reciprocal thunderbolt took on something of the power and the fatefulness of tempests. Since then they have loved without ever seeing each other freely. They have loved wherever they could meet. Never at Montreal, in the living room that Irina calls by its Canadian name, her *"vivoir"*; Wieland never comes alone to America. His wife knows of Irina's existence, and, legitimately jealous, she accompanies him each time he leaves Europe.

I have never asked myself whether Irina suffered from that perpetual insecurity, from that secrecy, from those embraces stolen in the shadow of a car, or the complicity of a two-hour hotel. I had never asked myself if she hoped, for instance, that Wieland would divorce his wife—she is much older than he, and he no longer loves her. I envied her Wieland, but gently, the way one envies a friend who is Irina. I have seen pictures of him, with his curly head like an old blond angel, and his faintly Beethoven-like ugliness. I envied Irina deliciously, but I never pitied her.

She knows things about Joseph that I have confided to no one else. She is the only one whom I have told about Augustin. But of her own trials she has always written or spoken to me with great restraint. When she divorced Clarke, she wrote me that she was relieved to have left him, and I thought her admirable for taking work as a dishwasher. But when she became a stewardess at the age of thirty-two I felt no particular admiration for her feat; she spoke fluent English and German, Russian, Swedish, and French. I never even wondered if she had had any difficulties to overcome—perhaps the hostility of her younger rivals. Then she met Wieland, and once again I took it for granted.

86

And now she writes me those words that any woman might write: "He has just accepted a permanent appointment, after having sworn to me he never would. . . ." And there is a sea of bitterness under all the other words she writes. It is she who taught me not to attach any importance to age. It is she who trained me to mistrust artifice and coquetry; she wears no make-up, no lipstick, no hair coloring, not even a brassière, because it lies. But other people go on counting the years that we forget, and if she is no longer an air hostess it is because she will soon be forty years old.

I have never realized that Irina was alone. . . . Could Irina— Irina, too . . .

No! not Irina! Thank you, my God! Not Irina! I was right to trust in her. Today there was another letter in which she asks pardon for having written me in a moment of depression: "It is Wieland, and you, who are right: love must never mutilate one in any manner whatever. He was right not to keep the promise I had wrung from him in a flush of sentimentality."

Irina is coming to Europe in July, and will stay with me awhile. My life is beginning to blossom! Why don't I invite a few friends to the house for the first time since I am a widow?

It was because of Martin Champell that I met Augustin Costa at last.

It's a curious thing—the men we don't love are always the ones who unwittingly do us favors of this kind—"the irony of fate" is a good term. We were at the theater, and the intermission was just finishing. We hesitated a few seconds before recognizing each other, Augustin and I. After all, we had not seen each other more than two or three times before the war.

But I have not forgotten the red flame my blood was one night —that night. . . .

"Cousin Sylvestre!" he exclaimed, coming toward me with hands outstretched. When he introduced me to Madame Costa, a tall woman, thin and blond, he hesitated again. Very quickly I said "Sylvestre Fontaine," and still more quickly, "But I'm a widow."

"Pardon me—I should have known that."

This time we gazed straight into each other's faces; the ice shattered and we recognized one another completely. Glinting under the heavy lids I recognized those eyes whose color I was never able to determine. I recognized his smile: a light in the somber face, dark as wood now, and grained under the white hair. But the same eyes. And the same height—a giant beside me. He must be fifty-five or -six, I am forty-four. . . . Yes, I danced a whole night long with him. A single night. How little it is, and how long ago!

"You can't imagine how glad I am to see you," Augustin told me. "For years I've been wondering whether I hadn't dreamed you!"

Ah, my God, I recognized his voice as well!

In every life there are slices, as distinctly separate as those of a cut apple. The slice of my Corsican summers I left behind me long ago. Then there was the young-bride slice of honey; the young mother slice—the best of all, and it has the fragrance of milk. The "phony war" slice, and the prisoner's wife slice (a bitter one). Then the densest, the most profound slice, the one in which I felt I was tasting the very essence of my life. In fourteen months I have not grown accustomed to the earthy taste of the—widow slice.

88

And suppose there were yet another slice to be tasted, suppose a fruit were offered to me—an exquisite salve to my wound? I am still a woman, I—I awoke, stupefied: what had come over me? I am Madame Fontaine, widow and middle aged; Martin Champell, the chronically lovesick, was beside me; and before me there was only Monsieur Costa and his wife, emaciated but elegant, thoroughbred, sure of herself. She talked to me with that casual ease that I have never had, and the irrelevant idea flashed through my mind that the people who have this offhand tone in French, these easy phrases, are the ones who speak English fluently.

"Sylvestre!"

That voice. What is so special about it? Is that what they call a golden voice? Is that the supreme vibration, the sublime harmony, the golden Number?

"How long is it since we last saw one another, Sylvestre?"

"A quarter of a century; twenty-six years, to be exact. Good Lord, twenty-six years!"

"Why such a tragic tone? You haven't changed. You were so grave even then; you gave such weight to everything you said!"

I am paralyzed with astonishment. *He* turns things light and free, and time is nonexistent! One would think he had last seen me only the season before, and his voice is intimate and close.

"You remember what I told you that night?"

"You told me a great many things."

"This was one of them: that you should be called Colomba if you weren't Sylvestre. You had something wild about you, with your fierce eyes and all that thick hair. And in a white dress, the better to look the part for what you were—a first ball incarnate! When my eldest daughter went out for the first time, blond as she is, I thought of you."

"Of me?"

Good heavens, that's too much. I had not hoped for so much. I must have reddened.

Fortunately Martin is paying conscientious attention to Madame Costa. For once I am grateful for the existence of oil, knowing that in Martin's mouth the oil flow is less easily exhausted than in all the underlying tables of the Sahara.

"How many children have you, Augustin?"

"Four girls. A real harem, isn't it? But a beautiful harem."

And again that laugh, those teeth. Augustin's virility is so dazzling, so confident, that the fact of confessing to four daughters cannot diminish it. On the contrary! I recognize Augustin so fully, in that huge laughter, that I, too, cross the trench of time that separates us. I do not know whether he was, or whether he is, handsome. He excited me then and he excites me now. I know that he is very tall and very big, that the shape of his face is the line of intelligence itself—this I know, but nothing more. With people I truly like I do not ask myself if they are handsome. I cannot judge them. I do not even know if Irina is pretty. The day I first wondered whether Jo was handsome I knew that I no longer loved him.

Ruined, Mother had said. Madame Costa certainly looks anything but ruined—blond, very upper class, with that diamond necklace wound so tightly around a neck so thin that, by a series of uncomfortable associations, it evokes the guillotine. She is still pretty, perhaps younger than I, with the marked ageless charm of women who expect to please not only by their beauty, but by an internal strength which is hard to resist. I knew immediately that that strength is her love for

Augustin—I feel it violently; there is no need to recall what Mother told me: that she "loves him enough to forgive him anything." Confronted with those clear, deep-set eyes, shining as though from the depths of a well, it is I who turn away.

I attempt wildly to annihilate everything that has happened since I last saw Augustin. No, I was not wrong at eighteen. The same kind of thunderclap I felt for him then I feel again twenty-six years later, with the inexorable accuracy of stars moving into conjunction. I waited so long for this meeting—now it is here. It cannot be meaningless, this encounter that occurs just when I have remembered that I am alive. It cannot be meaningless, can it? There is no such thing as chance.

I have forgotten that the intermission is drawing to a close, and even that I am at the theater: the drama, the miracle are being played out inside me. The bell rings, and to me it means not the start of the act, but just the opposite—the end of the dream. I have played my bit part. The footlights dim. I grow cold. The star moves on. I fall back into darkness. No—no, not yet. "Won't we see one another again?" I ask. "It would be so silly to—"

"But we're leaving for New York in a month!"

How matter-of-fact that voice can be. It's true: he's been appointed to the U.N. Why should he want to see me again? The other time, too, it was he who avoided seeing me again. (But was it?) He grips my two hands. I fling my last bottle into the sea: "You'll find my address listed democratically in the phone book."

"Thank you."

And that's all. I am handed back to a man I do not know, called Martin, I think. I do not hear another line of the play. Again and again I recite to myself the same ten-line dialogue.

In the confusion after the closing curtain I look desperately for the Costas and I do not even glimpse them. One Mr. Champell escorts me to my home and kisses my hand. "Sleep well, my dear. . . ." I shall not sleep. Throughout the night I think of Augustin.

What happened, exactly, in 1933? Why did we never see each other again, after that August fourteenth ball for Napoleon's birthday? Was it my fault, or his? Can it be that the weight of a whole lifetime hangs by such imponderable factors? I must find the answer. I must know.

"Those Costas," they used to call them in my house, with all the contempt in the world. "They" were the youngest branch of the family and the poorest; in a hundred years they had climbed not a single rung of the social ladder. The little house that belonged to Augustin's father was only six or seven miles from my parents' property, and I knew by sight the enormous dark-haired boy who greeted me with a huge smile when he passed me. I liked him, from a distance. When I saw him more closely, I liked him even more.

How long a night can be when you have a single thought to eat at, when you have only these few mouthfuls of cud to chew over until your stomach turns with them. I am sick with melancholy, with nostalgia. I try to imagine that it is simply nausea, and that I need only vomit to rid myself of the distress, to throw it off with the heavy Crillon dinner. But no, it is not true. I should have to vomit up my whole self to go back to the freshness and the appetite of that lost night—of that lost chance.

I remember it all now. I remember that Augustin had seemed

old to me because he was thirty and had a quite important position in a ministry! I remember that he belonged to the Socialist party and that the word resounded in my ears: it meant anarchist, it meant excommunicated. I remember that, when I danced with him—the whole night long, and I was red under my white dress, my whole body was flushed with blood and with wine, my whole body become a heart because it was my first ball and because I was proud of my first dancing partner —I remember that I had the deliciously ambivalent feeling that I was skirting close to danger, to sin. I remember his triumphant atheism: when he heard the word God he laughed. Not irreverently, not meanly. As though it were an enormous joke that had gone on too long. And I felt guilty because I laughed too, once. . . . I remember that he talked not about Stendhal or Giraudoux like the other boys (what would the young people of my generation have talked about if there had been no Stendhal or Giraudoux?). But of Malraux who had just published *Man's Fate*, of the danger that the newly established German regime would mean to the freedom of the world; of the labor party he already dreamed of founding on the model of the English one. I had taken my first courses at Sciences Politiques the previous winter; I could have answered him. But I listened to him. It is not surprising that I should recognize his voice; I learned that voice during the length of a whole night.

No, he was not like the others. He paid me no compliments; he held me close to him. He observed none of the conventions; he simply touched my wrist when he wanted me to dance; he talked with great simplicity about his father who was a retired official (a very unimportant one). In his manner, in his words, there was something that I cannot describe except by the word "freedom." Paradoxically, that freedom was the very contrary of worldly casualness—there was something primitive in Augustin that troubled me and fascinated me at the same time. His way of drinking each glassful in a single swallow was the image of Thirst; his way of eating, just this side of vulgarity, was Hunger. And his laughter was the first morning of Life. He was the only one not wearing evening dress; he told me placidly that he had none. And his dark-blue suit had the too-short sleeves of a cheap ready-made. He asked me point-blank, "Suppose I used the familiar address with you, Cousin?" I think I stammered, "Are we really related?" and he did not insist. Once he clutched my hair in one of his hands—it was short and thick, all in curls like the Empress Josephine's—or perhaps he only touched it. Or perhaps I was mistaken, but I remember shaking my head violently, and I think I remember that he laughed. He laughed at everything in those days.

"Would you like to come fishing with me, Sylvestre?" he asked when the ball was ending toward four in the morning. "The day after tomorrow?"

I remember. . . . I was hot and I had drunk a lot. I had a little fever. Everyone was hot. Everyone had drunk a lot. The large drawing room was stifling with smells, gray with smoke, yellow with artificial light. But outdoors the dawn was coming up cold.

The break of day is the abrupt ending of the dream or of the nightmare. The first ray of light is enough to make the night lose its reality and become foreign to us, like a continent from which we sail away: each instant we are farther from it, each instant we grow more ourselves again. That morning, as soon as I saw *the other element* beyond the windows, my lucidity returned at a leap.

I—Sylvestre Costa—had on the night of my first ball danced

94

cheek to cheek with an unknown cousin; I had so pressed my chest to his that my tiny breasts seemed inflamed, they were so painful. I, Sylvestre Costa (elder branch, vive Napoleon, vive the pontifical zouaves!)—I had drunk enough to bring me to the doors of drunkenness, I had let him touch my hair, and laughed when he laughed at God! All at once the terrible shame of early morning coursed through me. Augustin's golden voice slid over my shame; it could not cut into it, nor dissolve it.

"The day after tomorrow," he repeated. "We might as well call it tomorrow, at this hour!"

I remember that his gaze was a caress. There was no more pretense on his part, nor illusions on mine, at that hour that blazed with light. In all my life as a woman I have never come so close to a gaze. And during those few seconds—as I swayed between a desire that I would not give a name and a fear which I was still less willing to admit—perhaps everything waited, pregnant and possible. . . . But it was daylight. In the growing harshness of that daylight the young creases in Augustin's face grew sharper. And suddenly, as if the light were working on all my senses at once, I became aware of his rough man-smell, the smell of a man who has been drinking and whose too-heavy suit is moist with sweat. The pain of my small crushed bosom and the smell of his body fused into a feeling of vague disgust. He smells common, I thought. Yes—that was the word that freed me from the sorcerer. Why shouldn't I confess to that weakness now? I was eighteen years old and I had never spent time with anyone but my classmates at Sciences Politiques; I liked refinement of manners, a veiled, well-bred "courtship." Instantly my nicely-brought-up young girl's reflexes went into action: "I'll ask my parents," I said prudently.

He laughed his large laughter, and probably at that moment everything was already lost: he must have felt that stiffening in me, that faint flight—and behind me the solemn, and for him hostile, phalanx of my family. (My parents never received his.)

"Of course! I'll stop by this evening to see what they say. All right?"

"All right."

When I woke in my bed at noon I had sobered from the fevers of my first ball and my first alcohol. But I wanted only one thing—to see Augustin again. When my parents asked me at breakfast, "Well, did you have a good time? Were you the prettiest one there? Whose heart did you walk off with?" I could talk of no one but him.

I still hear my father's laughter: "You're not in love with him, I hope! Those Costas are all pagans, woman chasers, and traitors to their wives."

And Mother finishing his sentence: "Just as they betrayed Napoleon."

They had spoken laughingly, unthinkingly, just to turn a phrase; they did not know how their words disappointed me. They thought Augustin had a surprising "nerve" (that was their word) to invite me on a fishing party. I insisted. They agreed to allow me to go, "on the condition that you're not alone with him."

"But she's the only one I've invited," Augustin said with perfect innocence when he arrived at six that evening, and Mother asked who else would be going on the boat ride.

"She's going to see her aunt in Bastia—didn't she tell you?" Mother parried smoothly, with her infallible presence of mind.

"Too bad!" said Augustin.

He was dressed in white and he was shining clean. I remember that the brown stalk of his body made me think of a tree's; something in me had surrendered when he came, and grown flexible; something in me coiled about that tree....

He gazed steadily at me. And probably, if I had had the courage to say "No, Mama, it's not tomorrow I'm supposed to go to Bastia," or else, "Well, then, let's pick another day, Augustin"—probably he would have recognized that impulse, that promise. But I waited for him to take the initiative for another meeting; I waited, wrapped tight in my pride, tortured and yet smiling, because a good girl does not let any of her feelings show. I felt like a vine, and I looked as stiff as an umbrella! He continued to watch me, and I continued to smile. I wanted to hold onto him with my teeth, and he saw nothing but that smile.

When he said "Too bad" again, even my smile went out. The words hurt me. They were the words of a boy who had wanted nothing more than a simple outing in the sunshine. What did he take me for? Then beneath the freshness of his well-washed body I seemed—I wanted—to discern the cruder, secret odor of the night before, just as I made out the shadows of thick hair under the light cotton of his jersey pullover. Something fascinated me in that transparent virility, and yet it repelled me. Why was I somehow relieved when he repeated that horrible, that miserable "Too bad" for a third time, and went away?

He never invited me again.

In the days that followed I called up all my pride to combat the memory of that Costa who was "already getting old, anti-clerical, a socialist, and common-smelling"—as I repeated to myself in a kind of chant. I wanted to convince myself I had

97

been taken in by him. And because I was very proud, I succeeded immediately. No, not that easily. I met him two or three times that summer—it was the last one he spent in Corsica —and each time I received that blinding smile in my eyes like a flash of lightning, and that heavy gaze on my heart, like a stone. He greeted me politely, as he had always done, but I think with the slightly superior manner of an enlightened man amused by the scruples of a young middle-class girl.

I felt ridiculous; I thought him rather cruel. But above all I was unhappy. If he had asked me again I would have gone. And if he had asked me to marry him—

My parents were not tyrants; they had not forbidden me to see the "impudent" Augustin again. It was he—he, who did not want to see me again. I remember that I was so unhappy sometimes, despite my pride, that I had to concentrate all my strength on the memory of the bad, the dirty little smell he had had that night, in order to feel a little disgusted—and somewhat avenged!

Not until Paris did I finally forget him. I was a student, I had friends, I loved a little, lightly and platonically. I think I probably played at little loves with all my friends—except with Höberlin, of course. I went out a good deal.

And then I married. . . .

And now I am a widow. The cycle is closed, life completed.

I am already ashamed of the night that followed my encounter with Augustin. In the morning, as always, I was whole again, and I laughed at myself. I must have been victim to one of those crises that Irina humorously called "virgin's dementia"—those brief and terrible spells during which a young girl crystallizes all her power on the barely glimpsed image of an overhandsome actor, or a stranger she will never see again. I must remember that widows who are still young are susceptible to it as well.

I decided to carry out my plan: to go out more often, to see my friends, to entertain at home again, to nourish myself on crumbs so as not to die of hunger. I invited the Höberlins to tea with the Rapps, Paule and her husband, Martin, and a journalist couple, Claude and Claude Bergieri. The last I saw rarely while Joseph was alive because he suspected they were Jewish (a detail which would sooner have incited me to see them, but it was not even true).

I shall not, of course, invite the Costas.

When did my senses come alive again? I do not know. Perhaps it was as far back as the day Eliane's father looked at me in that way—or the still earlier evening when Paule talked to me in that tone of voice? No, I don't know.

But it seems such a long time has passed since I was a woman face to face with a man—such a long time since I have become intact again. The last time—when was the last time? I cannot remember it with any certainty. It is odd to think that there has been, and that there will be, a last time for each of us. Just as there was a first time. We don't forget that one, as the song says. But we never speak of the last. Do they remember it, those old men I see sitting on benches along the avenue, their hands crossed on their canes in the timeless attitude which, God knows why, reminds me of Homer? Those old women with white chin hairs who belong to the Association of Christian Widows and who have nothing feminine about them now but their clothes—do they remember it? I still think about it; I am thinking of it again. But I cannot recall the last time.

99

The Society finally closed down two weeks ago. My anxiety runs over now, where before it was contained by the schedule of regular duties. I avoid looking into myself—the emptiness would make me giddy. Jean-Christophe writes me rarely; he is at sea. In preparation for my tea I scour the apartment furiously. No! I do not want to, I will not wait till November to work; I will accept the first position I am offered, even if it is inferior to my title as General Secretary of the Four Cardinal Points Society. Otherwise something terrible will happen, I don't know yet what. I think about Augustin—very intelligently, but I think about him. I was curious to know where he lived, and I had trouble finding his address. It was Höberlin who finally told me. Since he always knows everything, he informed me at the same time that Augustin's eldest daughter had just married "into the aristocracy." That's really too much!

What moved me most was perhaps that very silly thing: that he remembered my white dress. Did he love me the night of that ball, that night as lost in the depths of time as a needle in sand? How he held me to him! How he gazed at me! How sweetly he spoke to me! But all that is probably meaningless. He must have loved so many times! But has he loved as often as they say? I do not know him . . . I do not know him. . . . Yet he remembered my white dress. So he must remember everything. The memory of that dress throws a romantic bridge across from the one to the other of our encounters; it is the white veil that binds two continents across an ocean.

As I reckon it, I have not had many evening dresses since that one—fewer than I have had nightgowns or bathrobes; large items of good quality last longer than their owners. (I realized with a sense of poignancy how fragile we are, when

I saw Mother give my father's evening suit, all intact, to the Sisters of St. Vincent de Paul, for them to clothe their indestructible little old men.) The year I was married I had a black evening dress; and after the interminable mourning of the war, I bought the one from Marion Rapp which for the past six months has been hanging in a secondhand shop. That's all. How short a life is! How few festival days and dancing nights we have! Happy nights, I mean, and fulfilled days.

I do not remember Augustin's comparing me to Colomba that night. But what is important is that for him I was the passionate dark-haired Corsican girl in the Mérimée tale. People always compare me to such diverse models that I wonder if I haven't a certain fundamental insignificance that tempts them each to superimpose his own mirage on me. Augustin said Colomba. Mother always called me Empress Josephine; Joseph compared me—in the early days of our marriage—to Madame Récamier, which flattered but did not convince me. Martin claims (and this is the strangest of all) that I have the coloring of a blonde. Whatever country I visit, I am told that I look like a native. In Italy it is not surprising, but in America—

"Where do you come from?" asked the taxi driver who took me to the women's club.

"Paris."

"Which one?"

"France."

"But you look just like an American girl!"

"Thank you."

They do the same when it comes to my character. To Irina I am French wisdom incarnate. The Fontaine family considers me excitable, a hothead, an insolent nonconformist. To Höberlin, on the other hand, I am a bouquet of artificial flowers, of carefully nurtured conventions. Mother thinks I resemble my father, who before his conversion could be violent and somewhat cynical. But Jean-Christophe loves my "idealism." I am a society woman to Paule, but Marion thinks me an intellectual. Actually, no one knows anything about it, and I least of all.

Still, it does seem to me that I have a certain malleability; I submit to various influences, to the point where I change according to the person I meet (though I do resist others when I sense them to be inimical). When Augustin laughed that night at the word "God," I remember that I laughed with him. "This is what they mean by evil influences and unsuitable friendships," I said to myself. But I was wrong. If I laughed it was because the first doubts had begun to corrode me, and I had not acknowledged them. Today Augustin's atheism would not frighten me. I have gone to the very bottom of doubt, and I know one can come back from it.

Plasticity was the word my school chaplain had used a long time ago: "Beware of your extreme plasticity, my child." Alas, Father, the child has grown up, the child has grown old. She has lost the habit of bending to each influence as it comes along. Somehow I feel that I should have neither to submit to Augustin's influence nor to reject it, but simply to receive from him the confirmation of what is most secret in me. I recognize him totally, this man I scarcely know.

I went to take back my evening dress from the second-hand dealer. It was still hanging there, mournfully, between a sheared fur jacket and an old green hunting coat. No one had wanted it. In that unsavory little shop it looked like a deserted woman. It seemed older to me. I carried it off with a sense of victory: I had managed to pay its ransom! I was happy to own it again. It had kept the shape of my body, and I stroked the lines of that shape.

Perhaps it will be useful someday, who knows? Perhaps in South America? In any case, it will be my last evening dress. As I hung it back in the closet I wondered what Nadine could do with it after I died.

Since the taste for life has caught me up again I think a great deal about death. Why? Perhaps because we best judge life when we set it against our death.

Last night again I did not sleep. I lived my life through in my mind. It seemed to me I was seeing it from a distance, in perspective, as though I had begun another life. I saw the lines of my past from above, and I understood (or perhaps I simply remembered) why I had sincerely loved Joseph and chosen him, freely. And, recalling those long-ago days, I was finally able to accept the idea that neither he nor I was to blame for the slow death of our happiness. We were the actors in a drama which was actually far vaster than the two of us or our lives.

I already knew how important to me, at nineteen, was the fact that he belonged to the high Parisian bourgeoisie (the very name Neuves was a caress to my ear). But since I have seen Augustin again, I wonder if Jo's manners and his almost precious correctness were not reassuring and appealing to what was weakest and a little unsure in me. Through him, the man-fact had not the violence that it assumed in the young Augustin Costa, nor the demanding and rather repellent character that it had in Höberlin, who was the ugliest among my companions, the poorest complexioned, and the most thoroughly convinced of masculine superiority. In those days a girl was still a little frightened of her first man. The very word "man" flamed in me like the word "angel," but a carnal angel whose sword had the power to cut me in two. I had been struck by the story of a young Corsican peasant girl who went mad the morning after her wedding. I knew her husband well; he was a large boy, dark and hairy, who looked like an ape. A handsome ape. It didn't seem so incredible to me that the girl should go insane at seeing him naked! But Joseph's pale face, his reserve, his very name, Joseph, simply did not fit together with any notion of madness. His first kisses were very sweet; his first gestures of love more timid than my own.

So that two weaknesses entered into my love for Jo: the pride at moving into a milieu higher than my own, and the desire for a total safeness. In that, at least, I was not disappointed. All was very simple between us, and very calm. But I had not followed my instinct in loving Jo; I had followed the fine, clear line traced long ago of a destiny imposed on me by an elaborate past. The truth is that I did not know what I was.

But I knew my fiancé no better. I remember, for instance, that while we were engaged he was reading a book on the mystic number of the Great Pyramid. "Ah," I thought, "then he is looking for the world's secrets, too...." Actually, I soon learned that he read only through curiosity, or to teach himself; never to retain a message, an experience, or to feel a conviction or idea. He never examined the responsibility imposed by the simple fact of his ability to learn and to cultivate himself.

And there lies the line that separated our two interior worlds. My husband's intellectual world was the one we all inherited from the western rationalist middle-class nineteenth century. But I am among those whom the war uprooted spiritually and tore from the past; through a bloody birth it threw us brand new into an empty universe. It was inevitable, wasn't it, that the heritage we received should have lost its value, in a sense, or be made up of false bullion; since the Western nations had discovered themselves to be almost as poor, and more humiliated, than the Chinese: "Ye shall know them by their fruits." Alas, the fruit of the most advanced culture on earth had been the greatest shame ("the most ignominious in the world"). It was imperative, wasn't it, to find something else? It was imperative. It is now. Absolutely imperative.

As far back as the time of my one night's talk with Augustin a seed as indiscernible as the one that forms at the moment of conception had stirred in me. But the egg had aborted. Later, as a student, the dream of voting and of winning the vote for women had been enough to excite and mobilize all my passion and strength. Marriage, happiness, the child came, and I forgot all of it. It required the war, my solitude, Irina, and above all that defeat, to force me into recognizing anew a fact that I was to spend ten years more trying to forget again: that if he is not committed, the cultivated being is no more than a mandarin.

And I was that mandarin.

Thus I went from my (rare) occult experimentations to the study of existentialism. I felt alternately Manichean, then progressive; I agreed with Simone Weil, the most pessimistic of believers, and at the same time with Father Teilhard, the most optimistic! Thus today I move easily from reading the Bible to listening to realist ballads. Thus I am incapable of determining whether I live in the most complete internal chaos, or whether there emerges from my whole "intellectual unease" a line which might lead me somewhere. Where? It does not matter. Somewhere.

Two days before the "tea" I surrendered to an impulse so abrupt that I only saw the meaning of my act after I had committed it. I woke late, at nine o'clock. I rose at a bound and barefoot, in my nightdress, I dialed the telephone number Höberlin had given me for the Costas. My hand trembled (a romantic expression which is a poor description of that ugly, *clinical* shaking which is in no way different from what Eliane's father has). From that symptom I could see how much the year I had just lived through had worn away my nervous resistance; and from that realization I drew new strength. Besides, what wrong was there in seeing the Costas again?

The ring reverberated in my ear. Once . . . twice . . . I am sure that I am going to hear his voice. At nine in the morning women like his wife are in their baths or in their beds. It will be extraordinary to hear that voice, and to find it there at the end of the wire as if I held the tip of a chain attached to him: it will be as amazing as finding a needle in the desert! Three times. . . .

At the fourth ring Madame Costa's elegant voice answers. Her clear tones fall like icy drops into my ear: "My husband has already left! Saturday? I'm terribly sorry, I'll be taking my daughters to the concert, and I think Augustin is busy. Yes, I'll give him the message. Yes, of course; he'll telephone you this evening. Or tomorrow morning." She speaks with absolute assurance and simplicity, and vengefully I tell myself that my laborite cousin's wife is the very epitome of the society woman.

Naturally, he did not telephone. Once again caught up in

full virginal madness, I waited for hours by the telephone. When I went to the hairdresser, Saturday morning—knowing quite well it was all over—I asked Madame Bouquet to listen for the phone. That was my last attack; in the afternoon I had at last given up hope. I was tranquil as I prepared for the tea. Remember, I told myself (talking aloud as has become my habit lately), remember: a lonely woman is prey to her dreams, victim of her nerves—her eye is open to mirages, her ear sensitive to the sighs of ghosts. . . . Remember that love in the life of a woman your age is a miracle, and not a right. . . . It is a fluke, an autumn caprice, and no longer a fruit natural to the season—remember!

I was contented among my friends. Martin arrived first, then the Claude Bergieris. They are both journalists; he is a novelist besides. She is the one who travels over the world while he stays in Paris and superintends the children's upbringing. She is beautiful, brilliant, and gay; he, with his crooked face and his intelligent eyes, looks exactly like an intellectual boxer—but a boxer who is resigned to losing ahead of time, and whose lucid sadness impresses me.

He tells me about his difficulties in trying to separate himself from daily reality, to work on a novel, while his wife is in India and one of his children is sick; I feel a little sorry for him. Actually, I pity him less than I envy his wife; I love to see women with that aura of splendor, I love to see them brandish the banner of complete success. But when he offers to take me to the theater, I accept immediately; Martin will be leaving soon and I will be alone again. I must go out. Particularly with men. It's a question of health.

And then everyone else arrived. Oh, I love that noise, the

people, the smells that fill my apartment! Life takes me in its arms again and carries me away.

I am quite aware that my party is not perfect. But this time I am not worrying about what the little matron will think. I've done my best, and that's it. If it is not good enough for my friends, then they are not friends. They have come to see *me*, and we have gathered simply to be together. I open the door myself, and instead of whisky or champagne, I serve tea and an apéritif from the delicatessen. I am wearing a light-colored dress from before my mourning period. I no longer have the means to follow the fashion season by season, and it does not bother me. I am proud of having paid for everything myself and alone: the flowers, the cigarettes, my humble little sandwiches. Nor do I mind when Annie and Marion open their eyes wide at my first white hairs.

Oh, let them stare, let them count them, let each of them think "If only I could take Madame Fontaine in hand!" I had heard Annie say that about one of her friends, once very beautiful, who was neglecting herself. And it was true that Gloria neglected herself. (But she was a ski champion, which gave her the right as far as I was concerned to wear her hair wild; it excused that cracked skin and the deep lines, each of which was for me the symbol of some deadly crevasse!) And it is true that I have some white hair. What is annoying, with Annie and Marion, is that they are always right, because their system is entirely closed, and the territory where they reign is entirely sure. I am beaten before I even start. Heretofore I would try to equal them by using the same weapons. The very thought that they might find me "not feminine" gave me such an inferiority complex that I outdid them at their own game. Now . . .

Oh, now let them pity me if they like! I no longer need them. I have crossed to the other side of the frontier, into the pure hard world where women present themselves unprotected, weaponless, and their faces bare. I earn my living; for that reason I have the right to live as I want. I would even have the right to be ugly if I wanted, just as men do. (It's said they have no need to be handsome, which is of course untrue.) My youth lies somewhere else, Annie. It is in the action I performed two days ago in lifting the phone to call Augustin.

I am astonished to find myself so strong. Strong enough to impose on the others the presence of Paule, whom marriage has not yet made beautiful, and of Léon. He looks like a young derelict—more heavily bearded, more unhealthy than ever, swimming in an old jacket. In a few days the poor boy will be going into the hospital. But I like watching Paule introduce her husband unaffectedly, and show Marion the secondhand ring that proclaims her estate as insolently as I announce my new condition by opening the bottle of apéritif. As I serve, I listen to the fantastic, improbable, and yet true conversation between Marion Rapp and Annie Höberlin. Marion's high, perky voice seems the extension of her long and pretty legs; Annie's large one is the voice of a woman in the habit of commanding six children—a sergeant's voice.

Marion: Did I tell you I met your friend Gloria—hasn't she aged terribly!

Annie: Yes, her skin is turning to leather, and it's her own fault. She insists on skiing all winter long without having it taken care of. At fifty that's suicide. She'll end up with parchment skin like a mummy.

Marion: Where will you spend your vacation this summer, Annie?

Annie: Practically speaking, nowhere: I'll go with Georges to Divonne for three weeks, as we do every year, but I don't call a cure a vacation. Then two weeks with his parents in Beauce, with the children.

Marion: I'll have practically no vacation either; in August we work on the collection. I won't go away till October—two weeks of hunting and that's it. Where can you go, anyway? The Riviera is jammed with the three-weeks-with-pay crowd, and Italy and Spain are filled with terrible French people.

Annie: And do you know why? Georges' family live way out in the country. Well, the Beauce people have taken a shine to traveling, and carloads of farmers are pouring into the hotels in both those countries. It's a sign of the times: the gold pieces are coming out of the woolen stockings and the mattresses.

Pierrot: Unfortunately for me, those women don't buy dresses!

Annie: What will your fashion be this year?

Pierrot: No fashion. Dresses created by the body itself: molded hips, rounded bosoms. All my dresses will shout "Come touch me, men!" You know, you've got to think about men if you want to dress women.

The kind of talk that makes me shudder. I was so glad to see my friends again—and now I am using them to measure how far I've come along a road that plunges farther and farther into the absolute intransigence of solitary people. Fortunately, Höberlin, who until then had been talking oil with Martin, came over to me and unwittingly played my savior once again.

"I've saved her my little surprise till the end," he said, speaking of me in the third person as he often does. "Cordobal likes Costa."

Excitement surges in me—"You've heard from him? You know something?"

"Nothing more—just that he likes your picture. Having emerged from the common people, he has always attached greater importance to class than to beauty."

"Thank you, and aside from that, old George?"

"Nothing. We'll talk about it again in September."

He grants me a faintly condescending smile of congratulation, as if I had just passed an examination. And it's true I'm pleased at having pleased Cordobal.

"But what about Monsieur Cordobal, what's he like? How old? What kind of person is he?"

"He is ageless," Höberlin says, "and I've never known him to change. If I wanted to describe him, I would say that he is a man. That's all. Whether he were fifty or seventy would make no difference. He'll fly his airplane and lay women until the day he dies."

"What does he look like?"

"He has a man's ugliness," says Höberlin. And for the first time I hear respect in his voice.

When the Rapps and the Höberlins leave, I have a vague sense that I have just carried off my first victory as a widow: unwittingly I have become that free woman, that woman who earns her own living, and who no longer has anything in common with the young matrons like Annie nor the young masters like Pierrot.

Almost everyone had left when Augustin rang. I found myself face to face with him. He took my two hands in his, as always. He said, "You're not going to send the last-minute guest back out into the cold and the dark, are you?"

I was stupefied, and at the same time I felt it completely natural to see him there, in my house, for the first time. Perhaps for the last time.

Why for the last time? He came. He is here. Everything is beginning again. Everything can begin again. I need only look at him to see that the long-ago harmony still exists, and that the current moves between us. Handsome? ugly? old? young? what do they mean? What have those categories to do with anything? When will I be freed from categories? Augustin looks tired this evening, the wood of his face is heavily grained; but if youth is no longer in his features, it lives on and it triumphs in his gaze, the voice, the lips. How absurd to define our age by the revolutions the earth makes around the sun! Age is the sign of time on us. Who would dare to claim that time flows at the same rhythm for all of us? Irina is right.

Augustin excites me so that I am afraid of betraying myself. But why should I be afraid? Oh, this time, at least, let me fear nothing but losing him! I am no longer the little girl who held a treasure in her hands and let it escape. I am a woman. And I am free. But he is not. My God! My God, what am I thinking? What am I ready to do? With all my will I call up my old morality, my old conscience—and I find only wisps, as if my conscience and my will had evaporated. I introduce him to my friends, I offer him a drink, as the ritual requires. But already I have turned into the wild woman of the night; I move in another world, I have touched on the fiery star. . . .

He looks at me, and the slit of his eyes lets his secret show through, and his smile affects me like a lantern I light myself by. The attraction a man exercises on a woman is like nothing else. Or perhaps . . . yes, like a heavy wind that opens a path through a forest of leaves, turning them aside one after another, slowly, with an enormous sigh: each leaf begins to breathe with the breath of that wind, it shudders, it opens into two, tears apart, closes again broken. And it falls at last, struck by a fatal exhaustion.

Soon there is no one left but he, Martin, and the Bergieris. We talk about oil, Claude's last trip, her husband's latest book —I don't know. Already I have stopped even listening to Augustin's words. Only his voice. I would like to record that voice, and listen to the record every night. I would never be alone again.

The Bergieris leave late, and at ten in the evening I am left between Martin and Augustin, all three of us on my Directoire divan—cramped, happy, perhaps a little drunk. I have drunk enough not to hurt at the thought that Augustin leaves in two weeks, and enough to ask myself no more questions. And suddenly that voice:

"Do you know that I was once in love with you, Sylvestre?"

I do not answer, but I drop my head as under a blow, so that I seem to be saying yes.

"Everyone is in love with Madame Fontaine," Martin puts in shortly. He must be starting to understand.

"It wasn't Madame Fontaine yet," Augustin says. "Why didn't we ever see each other again, can you tell me?"

"You invited me to go fishing, and I didn't go. You said 'Too bad!' and you never asked me again."

"I must have thought you would always refuse. I didn't like refusals."

"I would not have refused," I replied. "But life is made up of lost possibilities—" I go on repeating, "Lost—lost—" and I cannot stop, I am a cracked record. My life is lost . . . lost . . . lost. . . .

"As hell is paved with good intentions," Martin finally interrupts, with an irony that rings false.

"It's sad to meet again after so many years. I've thought of you often."

"So have I."

"I wonder how it happened that we never met. Too bad."

The same words, the same voice. And inside me the same small wound, hard and sweet, encysted for so long.... Who ever invented the lie about "the mystery of woman"? All the mystery is in those cruel brothers of ours. They can desire us for a night with the fervor they would put to conquering a star—and then leave us to vegetate in their heart's darkness for years. And when they find us again, dead, exactly where they left us, they can say simply, "Too bad," as though it were an uprooted tree they saw before them.

"What life isn't lost?" Augustin asks abruptly.

I leap loyally onto the perch he offers: come back to generalities, leave the dangerous terrain of rediscovered intimacy, of an impossible intimacy.

"Do you believe in neither God nor man, Augustin?"

"I believe in man—it's the fashion. A sad fashion, but it will last as long as heaven and earth.... Man, and the good and the evil, the devil and the good Lord, all at the same time."

This time he did not laugh as he said the word. And as I look at him, I sense what his face could be in sorrow. His brown wrinkles are so deep that I would like to put my fingers into them. He goes on: "I believe in the future of men generally, but I am afraid that each of them individually can only suffer his own defeat."

"How can you say that to me? *You*, to *me*? A representative of the Fifth Republic to a jobless secretary?"

114

"What looks like success may hide the worst failure," he says gently. Then he breaks into laughter. "But the worst defeat can save a man, too! The only glory of our mutual relative, and I mean the only one, was Saint Helena, wasn't it? Do you know one of the reasons I was so glad to meet you? It's because you remind me of the time I had great plans, of my illusions; the time when I believed in everything—and in myself, too, in myself above all! You represent my youth in a way, Sylvestre."

"But we saw each other only once, really. Did your youth last only a night?"

"That's just it. The ball that August fourteenth is the only one I ever went to! I was a poor young man and I hated social things. And then I saw you. Just try to imagine the impression Mademoiselle Costa, of the elder branch, could make on Julien Sorel, with that dress, and those jewels—"

"I was wearing Mother's pearl necklace, and a seamstress in Bastia had made the dress."

"But it was *you* wearing the dress!"

"And 'I' who never said a word!"

"You certainly did—you told me you were a Bonapartist. Are you still one?"

We are laughing, our heads thrown back, suddenly so happy that even Martin forces himself to laugh. We laugh, we talk. (Thank God, the generalities are done with for the two of us.) There is already a meaning in our words that escapes poor Martin, whose tense roundnesses I feel beside me. He drinks without pause, he wipes his hand over his skull as if to excite the spark of some reminiscence that would unite us. I am an amnesiac finding my memory again, and it is divine—a world is being reborn in me.

"Two weeks ago I told you what had struck me most about the very young girl you were. Strange as it seems, it was the weight you gave to the least of your words! You would say 'Napoleon,' and it was a whole band of drums beating a march! I was already a little blasé about politics, but you'd say 'Sciences Politiques' and it became a science again, a pure idea, a civic service. You also told me that the world was already in the midst of the Apocalypse."

"I must have been a terrible little bore!"

"No. It was strange, that word on your lips. I laughed, and I told you that *I* thought the world was in the midst of revolution. Later, I began to think that maybe it was the same thing. . . ."

"I'm not so sure now that we've entered the Apocalypse," I say, "but I still believe that we've got to forego our personal dreams, and that it's a necessary sacrifice."

"I'm not so sure either that we're in the midst of revolution!" Augustin laughs.

"You told me, too, that 'France is dying from loving Empire furniture too well,' Augustin, and look at you now sitting in my Directoire room!"

"I am sitting in a Directoire room," he repeats, "and I wanted to found a party—"

"A labor party!"

"Ah! You remember that, too?" (The smile brightens the dark face.) "I didn't give up the idea completely until last year, you know. I honestly believe I did all I could; now it seems clear I could do nothing. . . . This time I'm resigned to diplomacy. I say 'resigned' because for me diplomacy is the end of things. A way of falling into line, of taming myself, politically. And, ultimately, none of it matters. . . ."

116

He has grown calm again, and he smiles. Too late! I feel an old bitterness in him, and great disappointment. It hurt me to hear him say "It's the end." We women always forget that we are not the only ones who grow old; we forget how much a man can suffer when he reaches the age of retirement or the hour of truth—when he can no longer disguise the failure of his career, the renunciation of his own ideal, the death of his dreams.

"It happens to everyone," he finishes with the same irony. "We grow more careful, more bourgeois with age; we learn what peace costs, we come to appreciate the joys of the home. We're satisfied with making our wives quasi-ambassadresses."

"And our daughter a marquise," I say to myself. Then I hear Martin's sententious voice.

" 'If a young man is not a revolutionary at twenty he is insensitive; if he is not a reactionary at forty he is unintelligent.' Then what would we think of the man our age who had not tamed down politically and socially? We've all gone through the same thing," he concludes complacently, as if he had managed to reduce Augustin to his own size.

But I don't want that formula to be true—no! I want it to be a lie! The higher a man rises on the ladder of values ("There where the spirit, with your guidance, advances in the endless widening of thought and of action"), and the more he expands his heart and his mind, the more intolerable he finds the mystery of suffering, and the higher he strains his hands toward his mute God. I cannot help saying this, in order to thrust Martin outside the circle that holds Augustin and me, so long after our one night's partnership.

"Aren't I right, Augustin?"

"Theoretically, yes. Practically speaking, you may not

know how hard it is to follow to its end the line a man sets down for himself at the age of twenty-five, later when everything works against it: external circumstances, yes, but the opinions of his own wife, too, and his children's future. When a man has four daughters, he is compelled to see his career as a trade rather than as an ideal; he's got to court success, and connections, all of it. . . . How can you sacrifice living beings to ideas, I ask you? Even in my own home, I'm a minority! One poor man all alone in the midst of his harem! You can see how you really *are* my youth—you're the only one who remembers all my illusions." He burst into laughter, and was suddenly silent.

My body is a single sigh. He said, "His wife's opinions," "I'm a minority." Then he is separated from his wife by the same abyss that separated me from my husband. And I thought myself a unique case! What a discovery! How sweet it is! Perhaps Augustin needs me? Perhaps, with him, I might have followed my own deep vocation, I might have worked out my famous convictions without feeling guilt, and have helped him to serve his own. Perhaps I, too, might have realized not only my love but my true life, my human life. That must be what I had foreseen at eighteen: something more than a simple attraction between us. Something a thousand times more rare. You were too wise, Sylvestre Costa! If you had been less wise, you would have dared to believe in the impossible; and the impossible, being grateful, would have knelt down before you! But there it is: I was wise. I had always heard Mother say: "It's bad for a marriage when the husband and the wife have the same profession." And I could see that my father was grateful to her for the repose she represented to him, and for her blind admiration.

I throw myself back; my body is an unfurling of sighs. The wind tears in gusts through the leafy path that opens within me, and all my interior boughs fold back. The wind rises again and I am afraid that my face betrays the turbulence of it. . . . The atmosphere grows heavy. This is intolerable—this smoke, this heat, the ground swell in me, and on either side of me the one I want and the one I do not want. Neither the one nor the other can understand why I recite aloud: "He who believed in God, and he who did not"—a poem whose first two lines are all I know. I look like a drunken woman, rolling my head and repeating words without meaning. But I shall always remember that excruciating moment, when I am stretched and torn between the man I love and the man I do not love. I want to kill Martin for still being here; and yet, from the depths of my distress, I am perfectly aware that Augustin did not even phone me to say "I will come!" and that if he had wanted to see me alone, he could have. But he would be content with making his wife an ambassadress—he said that, too. And when he speaks of his harem, it is not irony at all in his tone; it is tenderness. He claims to be "in the minority," but he must know that he balances four or five women by his own weight alone.

The conversation goes on over me. From far away I hear Martin's stubborn voice—"We're an old country, too old a country"—and Augustin's answer. It surprises me awake, it galvanizes me, because it parallels one of my own most fundamental intuitions:

"I don't believe in the aging of peoples. All the world's men are the same age. It is our social class which is old, and that's very different. But there are whole layers of the French population who are just barely emerging from medieval living conditions, and who are only now beginning to reach a level of civilization in technical or intellectual areas. Those layers are almost as young as the ones in China, and they're the ones I hope will bring about a complete renewal. For myself, it's too late."

Again he says "Too late." And this time I am sure of it—he touched my hair.... It feels as though he is running a single finger along the white hairs lost among my curls, perhaps to erase them. No, not to erase them. They are the lines of our life, the trace of our sad hours, the long furrow of the spaces that kept us apart.... Augustin's finger falls and rises along the course of time, along my white hairs. I feel a billion stars burst in my hair. He stops as suddenly as he began, and his caress was at once so precise and so furtive that again, as I had that night, I wonder whether I did not dream it.

At that same instant he rises to his feet. "Midnight! Excuse me; but I'm tired, and Germaine must have come back from the concert long ago. You can't imagine what a pleasure it's been to see you again."

Midnight—tired—Germaine—pleasure—oh! I have been no more than one of those little daily surprises that life affords men like him. When he has lost me he will say, "Too bad." He is unique in my widowed life, he would fill up the space in it; but we are not playing the same game. Why did he touch my hair then? He should not have touched it that way. Not that way.

"When shall we see one another again?" I ask. "You mustn't say good-by for another—"

"No, not for a quarter of a century! But for two years anyway."

Two years! How placidly he says that! I feel as though I

am drowning. The cable the helicopter dangled from the sky withdraws and disappears. Help me—you can't leave me here! You can't leave me all alone in this sea!

I try to put into my voice all that is in my heart and in my body—as fierce a determination as if I had built it up over a lifetime. "We've got to see each other again before you leave."

He looks at me, uncertain, surprised. The weariness of evening stoops him a little. But you ought not to have touched my hair, nor told me that you had been in love with me. You should not have done it. The finger that smoothed my curls, that shook me to the heart like a mine, the finger that re-created me—that finger did not lie.

"I'd like to see you again, too," he says. "But—"

"Come have lunch with me," I interrupt. "Here."

My voice vibrates. I have lost all reserve, all modesty. Martin smooths his scalp, embarrassed. I feel hard, determined, like a small sword that cannot be turned aside. This time Augustin is not fooled. This time his eyes change, and his whole face, its creases as expressive as a sculpture's. And what I read carved into the wood is an expression of withdrawal, or fear almost —in this man who is the very symbol of virility to me. How easily I can read that parchment! He wants to accept, and he hesitates. Suddenly I see that he feels himself in the same relation to me that I was to him that day twenty-six years ago! There, now, our situations are reversed and I am avenged, a quarter of a century later, for the scorn he felt toward the fearful young girl I was! Oh—he does more than hesitate—he is afraid! Afraid of my hungry eyes, of my absolute freedom! He senses a threat. But against *what*, for God's sake? It's only a question of a meal, and we are cousins. I savor the mean vengeance of telling myself that this time *he* is the bourgeois:

the sleeves were too short on the suit he wore then, but now it is I who am wearing them in the form of this season-old dress. And, suffused with a triumphant shame, a proud shame, I look at him as he looked at me twenty-five years ago, with a curiosity already near to irony. "You really don't want to come, Augustin?"

At last he smiles. His face is suddenly transformed. "I'll be alone Thursday," he says. "My harem will be gone all day to say good-by to my wife's parents in the country. Let me take you to dinner."

We arrange to meet Thursday evening, at Lipp's. Augustin is still smiling, but with an expression that bothers me: the slightly satisfied expression of a man used to windfalls. I can do nothing about it; my insistence has slipped something ambiguous between us. He towers over me with all his size; his piercing eyes survey me. My proud shame does not last; already it is only shame, pure and simple. Oh, it would be terrible if Augustin did not understand, if he took me for what I am not. And yet what else did I want, if not to prove to him that I had changed, and that I was indeed another person? Once the mind is freed, the body must follow, mustn't it?

But the plain fact is that it does not follow. I feel myself stiff, frozen, at the idea that for the first time in my life, in my exemplary life, I am making the first gesture toward a man. His expression—I don't like that expression. Is this the price of liberty—this fear in me, this sneaking shame? When a person is truly hungry, he is ashamed, Irina said. Yes. All hungers are alike, and to ask for a man is like begging bread. It is entering into the world where you have no more rights, where nothing more is given you, the world from which you must wrench your share by tooth and nail, in shame—oh, God, in shame. . . .

"Unfortunately," he continues, "I can't even come to pick you up; I've already shipped my car. In a sense I've already left."

My God, it's true! He leaves in two weeks, for two years. All my scruples are swept aside again. I want these few days. I shall have them. But that is all I shall have. A true intrigue, with no tomorrow, without return, without hope. I swallow a dry sob as he takes my two hands.

"Good night, my youth."

They are the last words I hear from him. Martin lingers. He stares at me; then he says, "A very superior fellow," in a neutral tone.

I say "Yes . . ." I can say no more. I want to scream.

"But I disagree with him on a great many points," Martin goes on. "His idea about the eternal youth of the common people is no more than a brilliant paradox."

This smallness finishes me. I explode, I need to avenge myself. I invent, I lie, I babble.

Fortunately I remember nothing of what I said to Martin. But I realize how sincerely fond of me he is, and how kind: my despair touches him enough so that he thinks of me rather than of himself. He takes on his elder-brother manner again. Oh, yes, no question about it, he's a good old boy scout, a real brick. But scout or not, generosity is generosity, and it's not true that charity is always an insult. He sacrifices himself so far as to remind me that I shall see "Monsieur Costa" on Thursday. He strokes my hair (he, too); he makes me sit down, drink a glass of water. I grow calm. When I come up from the wave that has thundered over me, I find him seated beside me, and I sense sadly what Martin could become for me.

He kisses me on both cheeks and I am alone again in five

empty rooms. Empty, full of smells. The ice has melted in the glasses; the lemon slices look like flotsam in the teacups. The curtains are filled with smoke. The ash trays overflow with ash and with lipstick-stained butts. I had forgotten that I had received my friends and that I had laughed, and been happy. I had forgotten everything. But the easy chairs still show the dents of bodies, and the carpet the marks of feet. I stare fixedly at a round cigarette burn on the polished wood of a little table I loved. In the disgusting rolled-up handkerchief I recognize Léon's suspicious phlegm. I am all alone in the mockery of party aftermaths. Madame Bouquet does not come again until next Saturday: dishes and housecleaning will be my Sunday. I had never entertained alone before. I had never imagined what Paule must have felt, for instance, when she found herself alone again in her attic room, in the stubborn smell of tobacco, alone with Néant. Oh, it is terrible to be alone. Augustin! I lie face down on the divan, a tea napkin in my mouth for something to gnaw on.

I was awakened there at noon by a phone call from Martin; he was anxious about the kind of night I had spent. An hour later he rang the doorbell and carried me off, almost by force, to a restaurant.

Paradoxically, he seems to have taken hope again, since last night. It's incredible! He was probably astounded at the discovery of how weak I could be. He is too healthy and too modest to be capable of real jealousy. In his simple mind I must have seemed a cold iron idol; and now he had seen me burn. And then, again, Martin is a positive being; the fact that "Monsieur Costa" adores his four girls—and that he is leaving for America—is probably enough to reassure him.

I am a coward: I am gentle and nice to him. I am a coward: I pretend to be interested when he talks. I need a friend too badly.

In the days that follow I do not "prepare" myself as perhaps other women would do; Irina turned me forever against what she called the geisha's toilette: hairdressing, manicure, massage, new dress, to meet the man one loves. "You wash and you comb your hair, and that's enough," she would say. It seems to me I am almost willfully destructive of myself during those few days. I sleep badly, I eat little, my face grows hollow, my dress will hang even bigger on me. But it is I he will love if he is going to love me, and not an image all retouched like a photograph.

I think only of that—love. For women of my age the last love must be like a cyclone. Between the tender love I felt at nineteen for my fiancé and the total passion I could feel for Augustin there is the same difference as between the lion cub who walks on a leash and offers his paw and the she-panther defending her last chance for life.

I ready myself for surrender with as much strength as I would have devoted to resistance in other times. Who could hold in an instinct repressed for so long, and now bursting forth? I feel like a large star with bleak, dead outer reaches that suddenly reconcentrates into a tight nucleus of terrific heat and power.

I repeat his name to myself all the day long, like an incantation. Oh, a sonorous Roman name! Oh, most ardent of the saints! The saint who knew the red flower of human loves, who wept at quitting the wife of his youth, who loved the child of sin—he is the one who has the right to tell us that the

125

love of God is better! The chaste saints do not have that right. Or perhaps they do—as the aviator has the right to say that he knows the earth better from flying high above it, without touching it, than from walking the length of its furrows.

And I know, too, I already know what gold Augustin's voice will put into my name. All the potential forests in that savage name he will make bloom with leaves and branches of gold. At the pronouncement of that name alone I will tremble like the forest under the enchanter's wand, like a sensitive instrument that picks up the least echo and answers a single note with the whole harmony of the universe.

I had written Mother a letter in which I told her of my meeting with Augustin. From her answer I know that she has sensed a threat to me: for the first time she asks why I do not marry Martin. And she must have been quite skillful at finding out about Augustin, for she talks a great deal of him. Between her lines I watch his portrait take shape—a complete egotist who married and has completely victimized a very rich, stupid, and beautiful woman—a woman who is, of course, faithful as a saint.

Reading that letter, a strange thought came to me: that morally, too, I am a Manichean, for I made not the slightest connection between my God and what others would call my sin.

It is all over. Everything was different from what I had expected. One should never fear anything. Nor hope for anything.

I reached Lipp's ahead of time. Augustin was already there, reading *Le Monde* and *L'Express* with his bottle of Perrier water before him. And once again I was struck by the rather

126

remote distinction that had come to him with age and that made him so different from the young man he had been. I understood immediately that there was nothing equivocal between us—that something was about to be decided, very clearly and very simply.

He clasped my two hands. "I've been here for an hour! It's eerie in my empty harem—all my women gone, covers on the furniture, and no curtains!"

I could find only a very banal answer: "Curtains are very important—they're the only frail barrier between the street and the home. When they're gone, houses are like invaded countries. I may leave for South America in five or six months, and I've already decided to keep the curtains up till the last."

I was sitting across from him. Dispossessed. Evicted. How alone we were! Our parallel lives had at last come together again in the infinite loneliness of major departures. Augustin stared at me. "So I didn't invent you back then. You really exist in flesh and bone! What are you made of? Time has slid over you as it does over stone; it's polished you—"

"That's because I'm made more of bone than of flesh," I replied, laughing.

But I was not gay. Augustin's gravity, my sudden shyness, it all proved that there was an obstacle between us. We ordered dinner. The restaurant was crowded, as always, and the wait was very long.

"Tell me. What kind of life have you had? Have you been happy, at least?"

I told him everything in a few words. I threw my life onto the table like a die; it took up very little space. He listened to me with that quality of attention peculiar to certain men.

"Actually, my son is my only success. But he went away three years ago, and soon he'll be married. You know how little time it is, don't you, to own a child for eighteen years? I have nothing left. I've accomplished nothing—I haven't even tried anything. It's probably my fault, of course. But I realized too late."

"Maybe you demand too much. My children are my only triumph, too...."

The tenderness in those so-simple words moved me. In encounters between old friends, or old lovers, the most poignant element is perhaps that instead of coming together to face the future, we join in memory of the past, because the past is what we have most of. Two heavy, serious, long experiences face each other, in wonder at meeting and at being alike. It is no longer hopes, words, dreams that are exchanged, but the hard and real weight of cares, and of secrets. Two lives ground under the daily millstone look the same—like dust. Gold dust or dust of ashes, what difference does it make? There was a sweetness beyond desire for me in talking with Augustin of our children. We are talking about things we know. We build that moment on the granite bedrock of things that have been, and not on sand, like young lovers. We know what there is in the words "our children": there is a world. The only world vaster and surer than the world of love. The only world that misses being absurd, the only world where everything must be. The only world whose dimension in time is the future.

"What are your daughters' names, Augustin? How old are they? What do they do?"

But he does not talk long about the "children," and something restrains me from asking too many questions. How well

I could imagine them, those very young girls raised by a conformist mother, and probably representing innocence itself to their father. Innocence—alas. Innocence.

Our dinner came. At that moment something terrible happened in me—something that had never happened before.

When I saw my plate, I knew that I should not be able to swallow a thing. Not that I was not hungry; I was hungry. Nor did I feel a stomach knot, as they say, or a lump in the throat. With any knot, or with a lump, one can swallow, and I love the simple pleasures of drinking and eating. But this time there was a kind of hole where my throat belonged: a well, an emptiness, hollowed out by sudden anguish. It was as though I had no more throat, as if there were no passage between my internal hunger and the warm external richness of the proffered food. As if I were cut off from the very source of life. Now I realize that my body, more instinctive than my consciousness, already knew what was happening and was already translating it: life and food were indeed before me, like Augustin; but between us there was an abyss. I did not know it yet; I was only aware of that feeling. It was so new, so terrible, that my face must have changed.

"What's the trouble, Sylvestre? You're not hungry?"

He said "Sylvestre" in the tone he used to speak of his children. Then my heart died. What was the trouble? He could ask me what was the trouble. I am not an artful woman—I have never known how to be. I said, "I think that I could love you with all my heart, with my whole body, my whole soul, if you would let me."

He pushed back his plate. There was absolute silence at our small table in the midst of the restaurant's clamor. We were alone on an island, and our two lives lay between us ready to be plucked. The silence stretched on. Then Augustin said, "I think we could love each other, too."

Again the oasis of our silence in the uproar. Oasis—a malignant oasis. If I had been threatened with death I could not have swallowed its venomous food. I knew already what Augustin was going to say. From the heart of my island I saw the continents of the other tables, populated with couples of all ages, every kind, and I heard their voices. How happy they looked! How easy everything seemed for them! How easy everything is for other people! How hard everything is for oneself!

This silence was longer. Then Augustin said, "But we shall not love each other." And after another silence, "You know why."

Oh, no, I am not an artful woman. I should recognize that, and hold my tongue more often. Let others read in my eyes, in the lines of my hand, as Augustin read twice in the lines of my hair. I should not have answered him. I said something vulgar; fortunately, I shall never remember the exact phrase. No sooner was it pronounced than I expelled it from my memory—but the meaning was clear: I was perfectly aware of the life he had led for the twenty years since he was married. Whatever that phrase was, it sobered me. For some reason I remembered at that instant that I had planned to mimic Augustin at a distance of twenty-six years, and say, "Suppose I used the familiar with you, Cousin?" Instead, scarcely had I said the other thing, the one I cannot remember, than I clapped my hand to my mouth. "Please excuse me!"

Fortunately, he smiled. "I like your frankness. But now it's my turn to talk. So I've got to tell you about my life? I don't think I've ever done it before."

He continued to smile. He smiled almost all the while he talked, but his eyes had deepened. All was dark between us. He spoke for a long time, and not once did the gold shimmer in his voice. I interrupted him from time to time, or answered him, but already I did it mechanically, without hope, for honor's sake—exactly as in a lost tennis match you send the ball back, from simple sportsman's reflex. With, nonetheless, the insane hope now and again that a miracle will happen, that everything is not lost. Then the bombardment of enemy balls picks up again, methodically, regularly: tick-tick-tick, no pause for the vanquished, no hope, only the melancholy glory of holding out to the end, your teeth clenched, like the goat that clings to its life till morning, but is dead all the same. *Vae victae! Vae! Vae! Vae!*

Augustin ate almost nothing. After an hour, maybe two, the headwaiter came over, took away our full plates, our full glasses, and awarded us a contemptuous glance. On the continents of the neighboring tables the wines flowed, the foods were consumed, people laughed; all was normal—a good dinner, a good time. And there were Augustin and I, starving and shipwrecked on our island. We could do nothing for each other. Our tale would be the tale of a misunderstanding, followed by a separation as stupid, as fateful as life itself—and ending in a last meeting as fruitless as the first.

"I loved you for a whole night, Sylvestre. Perhaps even longer. And I never forgot you. It's hard to remember exactly why I didn't try to see you again. Have you noticed how quickly things move when you're very young? They spring up and die in a tempo that must be related to the greater vitality of the body's cells at that stage. . . . I was still young, and I had all the kinds of pride that the combination of a social inferiority complex and a passionate ambition can breed. And of course I was a little afraid of your family! Besides, I should be honest. I didn't want to be married then; I was determined to hold onto my freedom. I was probably afraid of you, of the urgency you represented; and afraid of the expectation that would have taken all our powers to fulfill. In Paris I lived in a furnished room—but that's just a detail. I suppose that detail, too, though, or another like it, and just as absurd, must have been a factor—"

"And yet—"

"Yes, I finally did marry. Like everyone else. Or no—not like everyone else. When I married Germaine, she was expecting the first child, and we had been living together for two or three years. In my furnished room. That means more when you know what kind of background Germaine came from. We were married in 1938, and I think that without the threat of war I would not have done it. I've never regretted it, really, because of the children. But for my whole life I've paid the price of my weakness, or of my decency—call it what you want! If I've been a poor husband, it's not entirely my own fault. I feed on smoke, I live by ideas. Germaine has both feet on the ground, and definite ambitions. She wanted me to build a career, and I sincerely wanted to serve a cause. That's one of the disagreements that have weighed on our life together. Germaine shared my convictions less and less, the farther we climbed in the social scale and as our children grew. You know that I devoted myself totally to my ghost party. I thought—

132

and I still think—that this country desperately needs a non-Marxist independent party of the Left. Everyone knows it, or says so, but some mysterious inertia has paralyzed every attempt ever made in that direction. Better men than I have fallen at that hurdle. . . . Anyway, Germaine has always helped me; she worked as my secretary, my campaigner, and my banker. After the war I started again, sacrificing everything I had to the labor party, and again she started to sacrifice everything to me. But there's only one thing I can still do for her, and that's what you've got to understand. Because I've always done it. And because I'm doing it right now."

"What is it?"

He hesitated a few moments more. Then, his voice dry and distinct, "Never to put between us a woman who is really important to me, a woman I could love. That would be the only real betrayal."

"Suppose I accepted your not loving me. Suppose I loved you that much? Suppose I asked you to treat me like . . . like a woman you did not love?"

"No. Not you."

He repeated "Not you," and took my hand—mine entirely contained in his, like a seed potent with all things, a seed enclosed in his sheath. Our two hands were free, brought together like hand and glove. My hand came to rest there, like a ship come into port after journeying around the world. When Augustin took my hand, and when I had abandoned it to him in a gesture of total surrender, I understood what it means to "give one's hand." For all my body followed, all my body was centered in that hand. I feel sure that it weighed with my whole weight. That it held my life. My whole life.

133

One moment more
And death would have come . . .
But a naked hand
Came then
And took mine . . .

Did he know those lines of Aragon's? He smiled at me with
great sorrow. All that sorrow, all that tenderness cut through
me, more painfully than the sword that slices off the hand of
a shipwreck survivor clamped to the side of the last boat. And
he wanted to cut off my hand, he wanted to drown my life!
I stifled one of those dry, tearless sobs that hurt me so. He
clasped my hand tighter and said gently, "You have a fever!"

It's true—I have always had this peculiar thing, and no doctor can adequately explain it: my temperature is higher than
normal. I live at an average of over a hundred degrees. I am
sometimes so warm that I feel like a small stove, or a collection of cells ill adapted to life on this planet, as though I came
from another, brighter star. But no one has ever spontaneously noticed the dry heat of this skin, of these hands. No one.
Ever.

I was thunderstruck that Augustin should have been the first
to feel that fever that burns in me like a flame. Oh, yes, I have
enough heat to agree to burn alone, to suffer alone, to shine
alone on a dark love. The words Augustin had stressed—"a
woman I could love"—those words had electrified me.

"If it depends only on me, Augustin, I accept the risk; I
accept it all in advance."

He answered me gently enough to mitigate the cruelty of
his words: "I've already told you that it doesn't depend only
on you."

134

"You must be some kind of lay saint then! But I'm not! I want my share of happiness and I'm prepared to pay any price to get it."

"Is it happiness I'd bring you? I must tell you this, too: I have four daughters, you know that; but you don't know what a man can learn through four daughters. For a long time I preached that a woman should be able to do what she wants with herself, like a man; that girls should be raised free, and taught to think of love from the standpoint of pleasure alone, and so forth—in short, all the laws of the new conformity. Their mother thought so, too. But she fell into the trap and she never got out again. I was the trap. I don't want to be your trap. You are alone—terribly alone; I would destroy you by loving you, because you would give me everything. And what could I give you, Sylvestre? When he's had four daughters, there are things a man can never again believe, nor forget, nor allow himself."

I fought on, my teeth clenched, with the fury of the she-goat condemned to death.

"I accept all the conditions, even your leaving in ten days, even not seeing you for two years. Even contempt for myself. And even your feeling contempt for me."

"You're suffering already—and that's just what I don't want."

"How careful you are!" I retorted. "How afraid of causing pain! Are you sure it's not male cowardice that makes you draw back before the responsibility I would be? Are you very sure of that?"

My head was working fast; everything he had said was fermenting there. Wasn't there a kind of weakness in him, in fact? If he had really loved me, long ago, wouldn't he have fought

135

to find me again? And now again. . . . Then I was past shame; firmly, and quite loudly, I said those words I wish I could forget, like the others. But I have not forgotten them.

"You don't desire me, Augustin."

He dropped my hand, and closed his eyes. When he opened them again, I knew that I would never forget that gaze. Whatever happens to me from now on I will have had that gaze.

Augustin's voice was the voice of an orator who has been speaking for two hours and realizes that he has convinced no one, and that he has not been understood. "You have the right to believe what you want."

After that we were quiet for a long time. Then I heard his voice, still calm, talking, talking. . . . I forced myself to listen, to understand. Little by little I came out of the nightmare. I felt I had already heard what Augustin was saying. Once more he was speaking my language.

"Why be afraid of what you are? You mustn't blush at yourself. You want all or nothing, you are still looking for the absolute. You might as well admit you're the very opposite of what you're trying to be right now. You hurt me when you said 'I'm willing to accept feeling contempt for myself.' You would not have accepted it for long. . . . We both belong to the last generation of idealists; we've got to have the paltry courage to accept that. Why disavow ourselves? We've got to go to our death with all our weapons."

I repeated, "With all our weapons" as though I were saying, "Let us die together!"

There is a sweetness for a woman in hearing a man talk her own language that is like the sweetness of seeing one's country again after long years away—or the sweetness of freedom, I imagine, after prison. But a more carnal, almost unbearable

136

sweetness; for the body itself is caught up in the harmonious round of emotions. As I listened to Augustin I felt a satisfaction deep inside me that was not of the spirit.

"I tried to become someone I wasn't, too, in a different realm," he said.

"Exactly what did you want to become?"

He took my two hands again. It was not warmth that flowed from his to mine: my hands are always the warmest. It was a cool current of fresh water, a bright fire, a light. From the bottom of the well I saw a glimmer again. So I shall be held to Augustin by a bond I would never have suspected: a certain fidelity to a certain defeat. Alas! how did I forget that I belonged to the condemned last generation? I had only to look around me at these young women without lipstick, their knees bare; at these unsexed boys in their dark sweaters—almost all of them recognized and greeted each other; almost all were part of the young intelligentsia of journalism and television, of fashion and films—to understand how completely the game was over for me.

"A man's life is too short for him to have time to surpass his own generation, unless he is a genius. If I hadn't married, maybe I would have had the strength, the time, and the freedom to go to the end of the road. I'm not sure. It made no difference that I had a doctrine, a passion; I would have been the same man without it, and it's no alibi. I'm still a man who has always worked with his head, never with his hands. In a representative of the people, that's the great dilemma. But to escape it, you've got to be a saint, or a genius. Tolstoy, leaving his home to go and die destitute. Or Saint Francis giving his garments back to his father. Or Moses Prince of Egypt, going down of his own accord to the Hebrew slaves, and sealing his fate from the start by an irrevocable act—the murder of the Egyptian. But not everybody can be Moses or Tolstoy."

"I know," I said. "I can confess something very naïve to you—I tried to feel hunger one day. But it was a false hunger. I was playing—I gave myself to the game completely, but it was a game. When I think back on that day I'm ashamed."

"You mustn't be. Each of us does his best, but I tell you again—we can't get out of our own skins. You remember the hero in *Dirty Hands* who had never been hungry, and who had to be stuffed with tonics so he wouldn't feel nauseous at the sight of food? Well—well what? What can you do to get away from the equivocation: go to work as a factory hand? Join the Communist party? I could do neither one nor the other because I set freedom higher than . . . yes, maybe higher than justice. But that very liberty is a privilege that I owe to the few francs my father gave me—to the schooling I was able to get with those francs. I feel a little like . . . those Christians who live surrounded by material goods, honestly acquired, and by even more legitimate carnal satisfactions; they would seem to have the right to enjoy them. But they feel the need to justify themselves—at least I hope they feel it—because they know full well that the single absolute teaching is the one that says 'If thou wilt be perfect . . . ,' and they know that they have not followed it."

I could have listened to him (for hours, people say) for the rest of my life. His voice brought me the confidence I had ceased to hope for. I was like a paralytic who sets foot to earth for the first time after twenty bedridden years and discovers again that it is normal to live upright. Yes, I had lived paralyzed. I had paralyzed myself voluntarily, because I had not had the courage to set myself apart, to struggle—against my

138

own weakness even more than against my husband. It is so much easier to read Tolstoy and Simone Weil than to imitate them!

I did not find it strange that Augustin, my pagan god, should speak to me of those madmen of genius who were so scorned in my circles. How could it have seemed strange to me, since —yes, I know that I am turning about in circles, and repeating myself. But it is a matter of what might have been my reason for living, of the conviction that separates me definitively from my people. The conviction that the vital nerve of the West was cut when that double rupture occurred: the rift between a religion that had become almost exclusively rationalistic and the great currents of the mystical; and the parallel schism between a culture that had become the monopoly of a single class and the immense reservoir of the people's strength. So that I concur with Augustin in what logically should have divided us. For there is only one rupture—the one that cut the people off from all the wellsprings at once. Having lost contact at the same moment both with God and with the sources of culture, the common people were forced to find their own laws again, and to do so alone. But because the nineteenth-century West—the West at its apogee—made no room for them, they went much farther afield to find their laws and masters.

What does it matter if Augustin has gone only part of the way, as I have myself? I would rather have it so. Is it too late for us? I have always known that it was too late for me. Like everyone else I stand at the frontier between two worlds. At least Augustin does not imagine he has reached his goal; he admits, as I do, to a certain weakness. He does lay claim, though, to a certain loyalty, and so do I. He is loyal to freedom. I am loyal to the spirit. And just as the Apocalypse and the Revolution are the two aspects of the same phenomenon, so the Spirit and Freedom are ultimately the two sides of the same truth.

My anguish was ebbing already, becoming more bearable. I sat before him, my eyes fixed on him; I felt as though I were a huge wave, piled too high, that crashes, rolls over on itself, and flows to peace again, humbly at home in the level water. Then this is to be our only greatness: that we recognize our bounds and renounce one another rationally, for the sake of a beauty we no longer even believe in, and through loyalty to an ideal which may no longer exist.

When he rose, I remained seated alone facing the white tablecloth that symbolized so horribly that evening, my life, and the night that was to follow. Between us the ash trays overflowed. I did not know we had smoked so much. I raised my eyes to his, and saw again that everything was over. He stood, waiting for me; he was already back in his life, already gone. I knew—I would know forever—that he stooped a little at that hour. I could not make myself rise and break the last circle that still bound us together: that cloud of blue-gray smoke.

When we left it was raining. We had no umbrellas and no car. No taxi waited at the stand by Saint-Germain-des-Prés. Augustin pulled his raincoat around my shoulders, and we walked along the Boulevard, our faces to the rain and our feet in water. Dispossessed of everything, so completely! And yet not free! Not even free! Two old students shaped by the oldest school, the school of a kind of decency. By what alchemy had our times transformed simple decency into crazy idealism? Now I was no longer completely sure that Augustin was right. But that was the whole puzzle; even if he was wrong, we could not do otherwise. There was nothing to be done. We both of us bore the weight of the same heritage. For us love would never be as simple as it was for the countless couples we passed. And that night we passed nothing but couples.

I had known for a long time—since I have been a widow—that to a single woman the world seems totally populated by couples. But I had not yet learned that the pain of being an incomplete couple is worse, and more subtle, than absolute solitude.

But is it worse? Beneath my distress the austere joy I felt at walking in the rain beside Augustin took the place of all else for me. Whether he wanted it or not, whether he knew it or not, we were a couple despite ourselves. Augustin's gaze, when it possessed me for a moment, was intense enough, and I had caught it deeply enough for it to shine on me for years. Twenty-six years after his first gaze had touched me. We handle time the way we want to. A single minute, if it has been intense enough, can be spread out to infinity. I had had that gaze. I had had that touch on my hair. I had this baptism and this communion under the rain.

He took me back to my door. And from the way he lifted his coat from my shoulders, I understood that he wanted to leave very quickly, that he would hurry our farewell. But in the brief instant that the collar brushed my cheek, under the smell of the rubber I discerned a scent that I felt I recognized. . . .

I am no longer at the age when one recoils at the immense symbolic burden of an odor. I am at the age when one knows the secret of smells, the reason that makes them so terribly taboo: they are the most profound emanation of a being. At first we cannot bear any but our own; but the day we tolerate someone else's we are in the process of becoming that other person. With a twist only half-voluntary, and lightning-quick, I pressed my mouth against Augustin's collar. I had eaten nothing, kissed no one, and my virgin lipstick printed the exact line of my lips on the raincoat's collar. (Sometimes I wonder how Augustin contrived to remove that mark at his neck—the only bite mark of our love.)

"Will you phone me before you leave?"

"Yes, I promise you."

"But do you swear to?"

He smiled but did not answer.

"Can we write one another?"

"I don't see what in the world could stop us."

"And see each other again?"

"In two years, yes."

Then despair washed through every part of me. The physical wail I had held back for months rose from my stomach. I had been able to keep it down as long as I knew that it would not be answered. A wounded man, deserted and alone, is silent; he finds the courage to keep silent, because the sound of his cry in the desert would make him more aware of his abandonment. Once the floodgates open to this bowel cry he knows somehow that there will be no more wall between him and his pain, between him and his panic, him and madness. But let a doctor arrive, and he will know that he is about to die.

During those seconds when I was losing Augustin forever I realized that my last chance was gone and that I was lost. I had come out of this house six hours earlier (six centuries), wild with hope; and I would enter it again as alone, as untouched as a young girl scorned. My voice rose as I said "Come with me!"

142

And at the same time I knew what he was going to say, and, not to hear that word, I laid my hand over his mouth.

He kissed my hand and he did not have to reach for it; it hung clinging to his face like a plant to its stake. He had to detach it and give it back to me.

"My dark-haired girl," he said. "My still dark-haired girl. . . ."

He laid his hand on my head lightly. Oh . . . lightly. My hair awaited an already familiar caress (the finger that re-creates me, the finger from Michelangelo's *Creation*). And I was given nothing more than that touch, like a kind of consecration!

We did not say the words of farewell. I gathered in his last smile and I ran up the stairs.

One day I will know, I told myself as I climbed. One day I will know everything. Just as I learned tonight that he had loved me once, one day I will know what he was thinking at the instant when he *did not* stroke my hair; one day I'll know whether he loved me at that instant as much as I love him. Someday—but when? In another quarter of a century? We'll be sixty-nine and eighty years old. What mockery! With a little luck we may be handsome pair of old folk.

Why haven't I the gift of tears? The theologians are right to call it a gift, like faith. Instead of tears I flooded myself with water. I poured one glassful after another down my throat. Then I swallowed several pills. Sleeping drug, my only lover —I let myself flow free to you, my limbs unloosed, my lips parted. . . .

I slept for twelve hours. What else was there to do?

Well, I shall at any rate have received one orchid in my life-time. But it was sent by Martin. He had ordered it delivered the day he left for the Sahara and as I read his name on the card I learned that it can be as terrible to receive an orchid as a slap.

Augustin left for New York without phoning me.

So Augustin's appearance in my life will have been a single flare of lightning in my sky, a heat flash with no storm behind it—the single victory in a lost war, the successful skirmish that starts one hoping again against all reason. Like Champaubert, or Montmirail. During those days my cousin Napoleon still thought he could win the French campaign! But destiny was weary . . . my life is weary. The helicopter has wrenched out from my hands the only rope that might have saved me, that might have carried me off. Now I surrender to a mortal weariness. The bitter waters have already risen as high as my lips. . . .

I must forget Augustin, and it is impossible. His memory is a burn to my flesh. I shall not be able to touch myself without screaming. When my body awakes, and begins to flame, I am a spark flying about the brazier that was its source and will be its end. At those moments it seems to me that love, with Augustin, would be like entering the body of the sun.

At other moments I think that I have dreamed it all. Those moments are the worst.

The Rapps have started a new perfume line—Caprices de Marion for women, and Chevalier des Grieux cologne for men. When they asked if I would travel around the summer resorts to launch them, I accepted immediately, as though I were throwing myself on a bone. From the fifteenth of July to the first of September I will tour France—by car or train, as I wish—not to sell the bottles but to introduce them and distribute samples. Orders will be addressed through me to the company. All my expenses will be paid, and I will earn three times what I was earning at the Society office.

Frankly, it will be hard for me to travel the highways with samples of Chevalier des Grieux and Caprices. Not that I feel humiliated at being an employee of the Maison Rapp. I called Marion to accept, and I was very proud when she answered me in a manner just the contrary of what I should logically have expected from her.

"I was sure you would. You've grown so much more self-assured! I can tell you now that last fall Pierrot had his doubts about you. He had them about me, too, incidentally; I spent years convincing him that I could be helpful to him! He doesn't trust intellectuals or society women. But you don't seem like either one any more."

"And what do I seem like now?"

"Well." Marion's voice is higher than ever, hung way up; I feel like saying, "Come down, come down!" But it rises still higher, and I know that in Marion this is the sign of a certain embarrassment; when she hits an obstacle and doesn't understand something, she takes on her conventional voice, the voice of a woman with an answer to everything.

"Well, that's just it, it's hard to say. It's funny, Sylvestre; there's something about you now that a person couldn't really pigeonhole—"

Yes—I've been told that before. She's not so naïve, that pretty blonde, slender as a flame—my little boss. I am the woman who will never reach anywhere again. It is the symbol of that endlessly stretching road that frightens me. . . .

Many people—Paule, the Höberlins, and even one of my Fontaine brothers-in-law (probably alerted by Georges, who knows everyone and always talks too much)—have telephoned to say that the Rapps' offer is unworthy of me, that they did not understand why I agreed to do it, even for six weeks. Mother writes the same thing. Jean-Christophe is the only one to congratulate me. How could any of them know the night I am floundering in, as blind as though I were drowning in an oil tank? I have become a glowing body, and I must try to put out the fire in the wind.

And besides, quite humbly, I need money. My apartment is too large, and too fine. My rent goes on rising, and I must consider giving it up sooner or later.

No one suspects what material difficulties I have fallen into since I am a widow. This insecurity I live in, the perpetual fear of a new tax, the relinquishment of any unnecessary purchase, the already nostalgic fear of leaving an apartment where I have lived my whole adult life—all of this changes me more fundamentally each day.

I have begun to read the advertisements again, this time for apartments. The classified advertising page is the widow's breviary.

I have received my driver's license, and I expect to have my little car by the time Irina arrives, at the beginning of July. I am so impatient to see her! I have so many things to tell her! I feel that to talk to her about Augustin will give him some reality again.

Irina's letter brings me incredible news, and yet she does no more than report the facts. Wieland's wife is dead of a heart attack.

Irina talks only of Ursula's virtues and Wieland's grief. She is putting off her vacation and her European trip until September, and I understand her: there is something horrible, something indecent in the fact that this death is—from whatever angle I consider it—a stroke of luck for her. "I thank God that Ursula died suddenly," Irina ends. "If she had been conscious as she died, she would have suffered too much at the thought that she was leaving her husband alone." She did not write "free." But she can say what she will; beneath the determinedly detached tone of her letter I sense so violent a happiness that it awakens notions of murder in me. I imagine, despite myself, how perfect her happiness must be; it is as unexpected as a star fallen at her feet, shrunk to the size of a diamond, and only waiting for her to gather it up in her hands.

I cannot resent Irina. After all, she did not kill Ursula, who was ten years older than her husband, and had been sick for years. Since everything is unjust, it is good that sometimes, at least, the injustice profits the innocent. One must always earn Rachel through Leah. . . . I share in her discreet triumph, her unspoken joy; I share them in the full sense of the word, as though I were her elder sister. But I was expecting her three days from now; her postponement leaves me as miserable as though the last train had just come and gone, leaving me alone on the station platform.

And then, suddenly, a terrible thought hits me, a gust of jealousy twists my heart, my body, my spirit: I am an orchard laid low by the tempest, a forest of fallen trees. Why Irina and not me? Why Ursula and not— Ah, I did not know that such explosions could sleep in the heart of an ordinary woman; I did not know that a broken dike lets in such tidal waves! But suddenly I remember that old woman in Corsica, who read fortunes from dice—and I see myself taking the plane to

Ajaccio to find that old woman. And I remember hearing of those people at Lyon who stick pins in a photograph, where the heart would be.... Then I think that the power of the thought might be enough, and that if I concentrate all my will, all my powers, perhaps—

When I realize what I am doing, it is myself I want to kill. Have I gone so far? How did I get to that stage? I take hold of myself. I drink several glasses of water, one after the other. I cannot manage to weep; I plainly do not have the gift of tears. But one truth blinds me: I cannot bear the life I am leading any longer.

For the first time I ask myself whether it is not my duty to marry Martin.

A woman without a man is a woman without a body. It should not be very difficult for me to become a soul, should it? But there is no absolute duality. All the religions know that: the fruits of the earth are sacred, it is true; yet since Moses they proclaim that man cannot live by bread alone.

I cannot eat or drink of the fruit that I myself have become. It is Tantalus' torture carried further: Tantalus denied to Tantalus.

I must go out, I must see my friends. I still have two weeks in Paris before I leave with the Maison Rapp perfumes, and I haven't yet gotten my car. The weather is like Italy, a weather for love. I am furiously bored. I play tennis furiously, slamming at the ball as though it were malignant fate, reaching for it as though it were my lost life. I go to visit Léon at the hospital. I wait for Claude Bergieri's promised phone call ever since I read a newspaper article by his wife datelined Cairo.

Yes, that is the state I am in—I who for twenty-three years of married life never played once! I have come to the point where I await the departure of wives in order to go out with their husbands! (Or to wish for their deaths.) I cannot help watching the mail; yet I know that Augustin will not write me, and that the light envelopes with the tricolor airmail circle will bring me only the solid, decent thoughts of Monsieur Champell.

It is getting worse and worse. I realized this from an insignificant detail that showed me the degree of my disintegration: the idiotic satisfaction I felt at finishing off a cheese I had thought would never be gone! Finally I conquered my Camembert, I said aloud with a sense of victory, as though I had bitten into the very fruit of life. For some reason Katherine Mansfield's observation comes to mind—it has no apparent connection with this victory cry—that living alone, one has at least the satisfaction of knowing that if there is a hair in the soup it is one's own. And I realized with a sudden horror how easily the life of a lone woman reduces itself to an essential absurdity.

More and more often I find that I speak aloud, I preach to myself, reciting this kind of incantation: "Oh, my six hundred, soon seven hundred million Chinese—come to my aid, I who have gone hungry for you, thought of you, spoken of you everywhere and always! Come help me, remind me that I am a half of a billionth of humanity, and that ultimately nothing matters. . . . Tell me that I am a happy woman because I still have an apartment with five rooms, and because I eat cold chicken three days in a row when I want to, and a roast chicken on Sundays. You, disincarnate Hindus, so apart from this illusory world that in you and outside you you no longer hear anything but the single tone of the music of the spheres, the great syllable Om which you say sounds alone under all sounds—tell me that in another life I was a courtesan, that I have sated my body, and that I well deserve a widow's slow death! And you, the one God, God of Abraham, Isaac, and Jacob, God of Saint Augustine—tell me that you exist, tell me quickly! If not, nothing exists but evil, and the absurd—and myself."

Sometimes I open the Bible where my finger falls: the Anglo-Saxon myth holds that there one always finds an answer. But I come on passages that have nothing to do with my condition. The distinction between pure and impure animals: the hyrax is impure because its hoof is not cloven, and the migrating locusts are pure. A popular proverb like "a whip for the horse, a bridle for the ass, and a rod for the fool's back!" A despairing lament: "He hath made me drunken with wormwood. He hath also broken my teeth with gravel stones, he hath covered me with ashes." Or one of Christ's rare and terrible curses: "Woe unto thee, Chorazin! Woe unto thee, Bethsaida!" Once it was an apocalyptic prophecy rendered entirely plausible by the terrifying multitude of my future Chinese: "And the number of the army of the horsemen were two hundred thousand thousand: and I heard the number of them. . . ."

The irony of the responses given me seems absolutely correct. Each sacred sentence certainly corresponds to a design, to a scheme; I do receive an answer, yes, but it relates to an entirely different scheme. I read the notes on the music sheet, but I cannot translate them into harmony. My story itself is one of the book's pages, the great book of the world, the book of life—the one that goes on being written, line after line, life after life, cycle after cycle, galaxy after galaxy....

Claude Bergieri called me on the morning of the Fourteenth of July, the day before I was to leave; he had just gotten an invitation to a popular song concert for that night.

A lone woman has scarcely a pretext for refusing. I accepted, but the pleasure I anticipated was marred in advance by the thought that I should have to be up the next morning at six o'clock; I had an appointment with the director of a large hotel in Deauville at two in the afternoon.

But I forgot my weariness with Claude Bergieri. As soon as we met at the door of the theater I was pleased at the sight of his odd intellectual boxer's face. A well-bred journalist is such a rare thing! And besides, whether I like it or not, I must learn to cultivate my availability. It is all I have left.

Sitting beside Bergieri, I find the solid kind of pleasure my evenings with Martin gave me, but with less austerity. Despite his (well-hidden!) love, Martin identifies too thoroughly with the role of the widow's escort. Bergieri is younger, his mind is quick and active. They say his novels are not good, and perhaps he knows it, which would explain his lack of assurance, the anxiety in his glance. I think rather that it is his sense of inferiority in relation to an over-brilliant and over-beautiful wife that inhibits him from giving his full measure.

After the concert (which was very mediocre) we go out for coffee. But Bergieri orders one martini, then another. It is the night of the Fourteenth; an atmosphere of false gaiety surrounds us. In the street a few drunken soldiers are singing an outmoded version of "Madelon" that sounds wrong. I ask

Claude what he hears from Claude; I ask about their children, about his books.

"Claude?" he repeats strangely. "Claude? Nothing to tell. She has to write too much for the newspaper—how could she find time to write to her husband? The kids? No measles in the offing, thank you. I had a student come in to stay with them this evening. Me? It's more than a month since we saw you, isn't it? Well, then, I'm thirty days deader; we all die thirty days' worth every month. . . ."

I watch him uncomfortably. I can't recall his having any Russian blood! Isn't he from a Portuguese family? But, Russian or Portuguese, when a person begins to talk like that at midnight it means he is about to tell his life story. I am not in the mood to hear it. Don't bother, Claude: I know already that everyone's life story is sad, and that they are all alike.

"What are you working on?"

"If you mean my work," he replies with mock pomposity, "I'm not doing a thing. If you mean what I win my bread at, it puts the cost of bread at an all-time high. I swallow a turnip a day for the publishing house where I'm a reader, and I write a monthly column for a historical magazine—an unsigned column called 'Nothing New Under the Sun.' Fashions in female names in the eighteenth century, historic sidelights on the Provisioners' Corps, the tribulations of the rich in the nineteenth century, et cetera. . . ."

"But that's very interesting!"

"Are you making fun of me, or what?"

"I'm trying to understand, that's all."

"It's not so hard, really: Claude says a person has only to look at me to understand. But she doesn't look at me often—she's never around. In a sense she's the man in our house."

He orders a third martini, drinks it in one swallow, and suddenly I have before me only a disintegrated face with nothing left in it, neither tormented intelligence nor obvious animality. Bergieri begins to talk and he does not stop. He cannot stop. I did not expect that; he invited me out to talk to me—only for that. To talk. Does he talk to himself alone at home, too, and aloud?

"Nice, a woman like you ... so restful. A woman who doesn't write, and who listens. ... Mine never listens to me. She has no time. And how can I reproach her for that? She earns on one story what I earn in a year! You know what hurts me the most? I've never told anyone this. I shouldn't tell you. ... Well, it's that she has the same name I have. The same first name. It's what I call predetermined humiliation. When people meet me for the first time they say 'Oh, you're the reporter? Aren't you just back from Alaska? And I say 'No, that's my wife.' Can you understand how terrible it is?'"

I don't answer. I remember how I loved my name, Costa, and that when I was engaged I had decided to call myself Fontaine-Costa. I naturally forgot that idea once I was married. But I am probably the only woman ever to question the fairness of the universal law that takes away our names. The administrative formula—"Costa, Sylvestre: wife Fontaine"—has the ring of truth even in its ugliness. No bearing on the Bergieri case, really. None? Wait a minute: he suffers from sharing his wife's name. It's the same situation, but in reverse.

"You understand," he repeated. "You're a nice woman. ... I never expected that someday I'd be talking to you this way. The last time I saw you I realized that you were nice, and I wanted to see you again. I didn't know you were nice *before*. I was intimidated by you."

153

"I've been told everything else, but never that I was intimidating."

"You were, though. Because you seemed so reserved, so self-confident. That's intimidating to people who aren't."

"I know," I said.

And it was true—I did know, now. Oh, I knew!

"A woman without a failing, without a fault," he went on; "a regular suit of armor—a woman like that is so cold! Now you're only nice. It's funny, we try so hard to find the exact words . . . and the simplest work just as well. 'She's nice. Sylvestre Fontaine is nice,' that says it all, doesn't it?"

His eyes are the eyes of a drunken man, but drunk not only on wine. Drunk besides with that thick, stifling tenderness—I have often felt its vain hot flood myself. Yes, it is his futile love scorching Bergieri. It is Claude's absence, even more than her success, that burns him. I no longer need to fight against sleep; a stimulant stronger than coffee holds my eyes open. I had not expected to find the same expression in a man's eyes that I had seen in Alexandrine's mad glance. A deserted man! Then there are lonely men, too? But they are even less noticeable than the women. Why should the success of a woman like Claude Bergieri have to be paid for by her husband's defeat? Does that mean that there is not enough to go around, that there is only one share for every two people?

I would rather not look into Claude Bergieri's eyes—they make me dizzy. Am I doomed to lifesaving when I feel myself much less a life raft than a victim? But then perhaps everyone is the victim of some internal shipwreck—perhaps we are all phantom ships of our murdered dreams. I cannot look at Bergieri, but how can I escape that voice, the voice of a punch-drunk boxer, hoarse with a tragic irony?

154

"When we were married I was the one who was Claude Bergieri! It wasn't much, but it was me. Now it's her."

I put a cigarette between his lips, as you do for a cripple; I hold my lighter to it. He draws spasmodically, he chokes on the smoke, he brings his eyes very close to mine. I start talking at random, hoping that some stray word will offer him a handgrip, that he will clutch it, I have no idea yet which word, I only know I must talk, that I must not stop talking. I take it on myself to swear to him that Claude loves him, because I know through experience that one always loves one's husband in one fashion or another, and that ultimately, I tell him, "All the other business is blather." From time to time he mumbles that I am nice. When I finally ask him why he is no longer writing, I see something flinch on his mask: intelligence emerges once more from that mangled face.

"Why should I write?" he asks me.

"To comfort yourself. To say everything you've just told me."

"You have a very female conception of literature," he says teasingly.

But he is listening to me—he must be, because he is answering. I press blindly on, following the scent.

"No—not just female. Primitive. To my mind, ink should be blood, as some Hindu philosopher says. Oh—excuse me! What kind of novels do you write?"

"I *wrote* bad novels."

"Then I can go on," I say, smiling, "and confess that I can't read the perfectly-made little novels any more . . . nor even the great nineteenth-century novels. You see, I'm not the person you thought I was. For me every sentence has got to be a prayer, or an imprecation. You know, since I am a widow, so

155

many ideas have come to me, so many thoughts have crossed my mind, that I often wish I could express them. Writing would have relieved me, like crying—like screaming. I'm Corsican, you see. I may have some innate longing for their kind of lament. . . ."

"That must be it," he says, and he is smiling for the first time.

"I'm quite aware that I'm moving against the current. I listened to some philosophy students talking about it this winter at a friend's house—esthetics, commitment, detachment, and so on. They're right, in a sense, but I can't help feeling that anyone has the right to cry out, if a cry rises to his lips. Don't you think so?"

"No," Claude replies. "You're nice, but no. There are maybe a hundred thousand of us writing in this country. Which is to say a hundred thousand useless mouths."

"A hundred thousand!"

The figure suffocates me. I knew that there were too many women, too many widows in France, too many children in China, too many men on the earth. And not enough bread. Not enough money. And now it appears there are too many intelligent people, too, too many writers, too many books? Oh, I did not know that! Then who is not superfluous? Who is necessary then? Whose life is not absurd?

"And talkative mouths at that," Claude continues. "Insistent, bawling, voracious! Each one is howling its own couplet: 'Listen to me, I have something to tell you!' It's grotesque. Since I've started reading for publishers I don't even believe in other people's books any longer. I write beginners' letters like this: 'Sir: Like you, I believed I had talent; I have now given up writing after ten failures. I would like to spare you the same fate. . . .' Or 'Madam: You write bad novels to express yourself; go and consult a good psychiatrist instead.' I'd like to establish a league against literature. You see the stage I've gotten to."

"You'd be establishing a league against—how many did you say—a hundred thousand Frenchmen at the same time. But if even two billion men wanted to write, it might still be important to let them do it! Because, after all, each life is unique, each word is irreplaceable. Because everything may be necessary. And it's quite true that it would all be swallowed up in the 'ocean of silence,' but what does that matter? All of life moves toward death, every word brings on a deeper silence. But while we wait to return to the All, we've got to live, one by one, and express ourselves, word by word—"

This time the face is finally completely whole again. Claude smiles. "What is this—she's intelligent! And I had planned to spend an evening with an idiot!"

"And so you picked me. Thanks very much!"

"No, I picked you because you were nice."

We are laughing. Claude is visibly better now. I offer to drive him home in the little car I had picked up two nights before. We start off for the Buttes-Chaumont. We travel through the kind of night that comes after a holiday, and from time to time an isolated burst of laughter, the sound of voices try to convince us that there *was* a holiday. When I draw up before the new apartment house he lives in, he does not open the door right away.

"See that window?" he asks, pointing out a square of light on the ninth floor. "That's the student. He must be getting impatient."

"Go on up quick!"

157

"I'm going to be all alone. . . ."

His distress rouses my maternal feeling—I press a kiss on his cheek. I should not have done it. Already he is leaning over me; he kisses me. Not at all like his mother. And I let him do it, because I, too . . .

If someone came across us now, he would see two madmen, not two lovers. Two madmen impelled by two different insanities, each seeking on the lips of the other what he can never find there. We kiss the way people wound themselves, like flagellants, with a kind of dark exaltation, each of us slaking a rage that stays private, each straining to drag the other into a delirium he cannot enter. One of my earrings falls and slides under the seat. My feet hit against the car's pedals. It is sordid. And it is long. . . . His alcohol taste, my coffee taste, mingle in the monstrous alchemy of loveless kisses. Monstrous or miraculous—there is no middle ground; communion or sacrilege, with a universe between them. When I pull away I feel ashamed. Bergieri seems sobered, too. I know that he never ceased for a moment to cry for Claude in my mouth, and that all my body answered "Augustin."

"Can I see you again in October?" he asks me, however.

And despite myself I answer "Of course, why not?" Yes, why not? Why not? But why?

"I shouldn't think you were one of those women who do it as though they were drinking a glass of water?" he asks abruptly.

"Do what?"

"Make love."

"No," I answer. "No. If love were a glass of water it wouldn't be worth much."

158

"Sure it would," Claude says. "A glass of water when you're thirsty is the best thing in the world."

"Yes, but—"

"There is no but."

I watched as he moved away, and as he turned with a friendly wave. I drove home too fast, right through the warning lights. I left the windows open, so that the pure night could wash away the very memory of the scene that had taken place on that seat. I had to get down on my hands and knees to find the earring. As I closed the door, I glanced automatically at the dashboard indicator: forty-four kilometers. It occurred to me that it registered my age, and that everything was absurd.

I brushed my teeth as carefully as if I had kissed an invalid and then lay down with no hope of sleep. I avoided thought; any movement, any memory would have been a single name. I had no desire to drink water from Claude Bergieri's cup. I am not in love with him. I don't even find him attractive. Would I eat willingly from a stranger's plate?

And yet I cannot live forever without a man. It's not true that such a thing is possible. But neither is it possible for me to make love without love. Well, then: must I really marry Martin? But I do not love Martin either. What stunning trick, what sleight of hand makes it seem possible to do with Martin what is out of the question with Claude, simply because I would be Martin's wife? Why should marriage legitimize settling for less than the absolute?

Irina says that one has no right to bungle one's life twice. . . .

Yet I cannot simply go to New York, camp at the doors of the U.N., await Augustin's passing, and live off the alms of a glance, can I? That is romanticism. That is madness. Then is the choice between madness and frustration the only choice I—?

Oh, my God, how hard everything has become for me! Are things harder for me than for other people? But other women, even the most unhappily married, still have their husbands upright beside them, a sword that bars them and protects them from temptation, from the abyss. "Silly," Jo would have said. "Silly little woman!"

When dawn broke an immediate peace moved over me, as it always does. I turned flat on my stomach and fell asleep. When the telephone service woke me at six I leaped to my feet in a total release.

I am going to work again. I am saved.

I drive endlessly along endless roads. Once or twice each day there is a bad moment to get through—when I present myself and the perfumes to the directress of a beauty house or to a hotel manager. Sometimes I get an immediate categorical refusal; once or twice an insult. But in any case such moments are soon over. Most of my time is spent on the highway, or planning the laps of the trip, or finding a hotel. I like driving with a purpose. All the roads have taken on a meaning, a necessity. This is different from sliding down the great toboggan of the national highways seated beside my husband in the big black limousine. I used to be terribly bored in cars, because we might drive for three hundred kilometers without a word from Joseph. He liked to drive for driving's sake, he enjoyed racking up mileage, he never looked at the landscape, never stopped to see anything at all. I sometimes had the feeling that I was a prisoner being carried relentlessly off toward a destination that had nothing to do with me.

This time I bought an atlas; I consult the guidebook; I spread out military-size maps and trace my way through the areas I cross. I had no idea that such an immense difference of perspective would emerge: like the difference between skimming over a country in an airplane and traveling through it on a bicycle. The road had been an instrument of vacation for me; now it has become an instrument for work. That changes everything. When I catch sight of the first small town after a hundred and fifty kilometers, I feel as though I were watching at its founding—no, better, as though I were creating it myself, because some kind of capital was needed at the center of so much emptiness. I *will* a town to stop in, to fill the gas tank, or to drink a fruit juice; and because I will it, it rises before me, there where it should be.

Augustin's ideas travel with me. Revolution . . . Apocalypse . . . "All the people in the world are the same age," he said; and "Most Frenchmen are just moving out of the Middle Ages." It is true. All the scenery is still here: the Romanesque church (abandoned now); the horseshoe sign over the blacksmith shop (but there are no more workhorses); the château (but it has become a summer camp); the farm with its stone portal (but the last of the peasants, Pierrot Rapp says, have taken the first step along the road of their uprooting: they are tourists). The frameworks of the Middle Ages have lasted longer than all the others, and the artisanal setting will probably be the last to crumble; it has already resisted big businesses and survived the little ones. But the rift is growing and it is eating under the foundations of our cathedral. Another race of men begins to emerge from the flood and this race confronts the oldest French myth—the individualism of the peasant—with the inexorable principle of coalition.

But do all these incredibly diverse units, diverse in shape and in color—these bits of a thousand-times-patched coverall—do they only go back to the Middle Ages? Marx said that we are just barely emerging from prehistory. That is true, too. These highways still follow the paths traced out by our ancestors in the Stone Age; even before the Romanesque temples, these high points of land that bear church steeples now were the focal points of some obscure intuition, some murky fear. And these men in the roadside fields—their fathers were still clay figures half captive in the mud—Adams in rough draft.

Occasionally a car passes me at ninety miles an hour: a red Giulietta with Italian plates or a DS 19 with a canoe longer than itself overturned like a dead swan on the roof. The driver's neck is tensed forward, his gaze fixed, his hands clenched to the wheel as tight as if his life depended on the insane average he is determined to maintain (whereas exactly the opposite is true). As he flashes past I glimpse the woman at his side terrified with the speed, or else perilously excited with it—in any case she is delivered up to the driver's will, in passiveness or panic. Then in my little car I grip the wheel harder, I become an Amazon, a gypsy, a Valkyrie, a witch on her broom, a bird of the wide skies, a pilot; I breathe the wind of every adventure. In short, I have a fine time.

The kilometer count piles up; one morning the gauge reaches the figure of the year I was born. During the day I watch my life unfold on the dashboard: 1933, the August Fourteenth ball (Augustin); 1935, my marriage; 1937, Jean-Christophe; 1940, the cataclysm; 1946, Virginie; 1958, my husband's death. After that I move into infinity and time no longer counts.... In my memory my journey is a whole, a mass spotted only by a few snapshot happenings.

There is the morning I discovered a kind of sea dog curled up in my car in the hotel garage, a derelict in a middy who rose at my scream and moved on, touching his finger to his sailor cap. There is the time I crossed the line between *départements*, when I passed the sign that reminded me how close I was to Neuves. It was a day when everything had gone wrong, when I was weary and disconsolate; I felt an unexpected homesickness for our bedroom there and its *toile de Jouy* hangings, for the magically silent pond, for the inconvenience of the worn stone steps, and even for Great-uncle Fontaine's dictatorship. The nostalgia is mingled with a furtive sense of failure. We are never done with breaking off from our past.

There is that despondent time when after a bad lunch in an unpleasant restaurant I was so tired that I walked into a chapel near Albi—a low white Carolingian chapel where I drowsed off with my face well hidden in my hands, apparently deep in meditation. (I always close my eyes in churches anyway; otherwise the plaster statues and the electric candles would stir me to the fury of an iconoclast.) I was not remorseful about it—I have always believed that sleep can be a form of prayer, and that a certain quality of repose is related to meditation. Doesn't Nietzsche parallel Hindu spiritualism when he says "It is no small thing to know how to sleep; one must know how to keep awake the whole day to be able to sleep well"? And what is the goal of Hinduism but existence without life, the total reabsorption in the Being?

There is that stop in a truckers' restaurant in the middle of the Cévennes Mountains, and that driver with drooping mustaches who gave me his unopened pack of Gauloises when he saw I had none. Then he told me his life story (he, too! He is a widower, he was not happy, he has a good job), and asked me then and there to marry him. I remember nothing of him but a sky-blue gaze and an intolerable odor of garlic. But he paid me one of the greatest compliments I ever received when he told me "You look like a strong, brave little woman." (He had seen me wash and park the car and lift out the suitcases.) I have saved his address with a feeling of tenderness: Abel Couture, Garage des Lunes, near Saint-Flour. Oh, Neuves!

Another time it was my own idea to start a conversation with a beauty counselor whom I ran into everywhere, and who always smiled at me with an expression combining complicity and despair. Like me, she was touring the country, stopping for three days or a week in each watering spot, each beach resort, to give advice and service to the clients of the large beauty salon she represents. I was struck by her melancholy, and once again I played Saint Bernard and invited her to dine with me at Menton. It was a mistake; it was immediately clear that she was not looking for a man—not at all—and that she liked my type. I was very embarrassed. "You look like l'Aiglon," she told me. Well! No one had ever said that before either!

There is my brief meeting with Jean-Christophe at Marseilles; it is good to know that he finds me more "terrific" than ever, and to carry away his huge kiss like fresh energy. I did not wash my cheek that night, to keep the print of his mouth there longer. His "Mother" resounded a long while in my ear, like a conch shell, like a grotto reverberating with echoes. Enough! I would have been a fine faithful echo—I never lose vibrations once they have reached me.

Each week I give myself one or two days off in the towns where I have had my mail forwarded to General Delivery. Among the letters from Jean-Christope and Irina, from Mother

164

and from Martin, I watch despite myself for the unfamiliar handwriting, the foreign stamp that would allow me to hope for a second against all probability for a letter from— But I have sworn never to pronounce that name again, never to think again of Augustin. When I hear "Augustin" in echo, I thrust the name back into the void, without listening to it. Unfortunately, "Augustin" ends with a very common sound; a thousand words rhyme with it. Mar*tin*—Augus*tin*. Gauloise cigarettes, Gallic civilization, Gallo-Roman, Roman empire, La*tin* —Augus*tin*. Romanesque chapel built under Charlemagne, Charlemagne the emperor, Emperor Augustus—Augustin. But I have sworn not to think about Augustin, never to pronounce the name Augustin. I never say "Augustin."

During my days off there is such an immense fatigue to slough off that fortunately I do not think about anything at all. I need a whole day to untense, to quiet the sound of the motor humming in my head, the ship rhythm that makes me pitch, the abnormal fever that burns my skin. The second day is delicious.

I am so thin and my appearance is so austere: white and black, like a widow from birth, perhaps, or a keyboard condemned to eternal silence—that no one ever believes me when I say one very simple thing: that my greatest satisfactions have come to me through my body. Whatever I know of happiness I have learned through it. But of all bodily sensations—apart from those one does not mention—I think I like best the one of total relaxation at the border of sleep and consciousness. I have always loved the sensuality of my bed and the act of absolute release I feel at the very moment of dropping into sleep.

Last year I learned what depth the well of repose can reach. When I came to my mother's house in Corsica, six weeks after Joseph's death, I was still stunned by a monstrous shock; I was empty of all substance. For more than three months I did nothing but relearn sleep, appetite, the normal rhythm of days and nights. But each of us has felt this; there are days when, after an exhaustion that seemed destined to go on forever, rest is a paradise in which each tension gives way, each limb is transfigured, each burned-out cell revives. Then something inside us stops beating, roiling, clamoring. And the ecstatic body gently learns to recognize itself, to find itself again in the new shape that emerges slowly from its wreckage.

In my bath I flutter my limbs to distract them from their weariness; I turn the water flow over them in a kind of ritual anointment; I stay in the tub till I feel wet to the heart, turned to liquid myself. Then clean lingerie, a freshly pressed dress. Then, with my hair washed clean and still undone, I begin my real rest, the superfluous rest of a body that already feels equipped to suffer its daily wear. I surrender myself to rest, as you surrender to the sun, to sleep, perhaps to death. I drink up this repose, and each throatful recalls me to life, restores me like a transfusion. Soon I am nothing but repose; soon the last faint, dying sensation of fatigue turns suddenly into a sensation of strength, of power gathering before an effort, and of a leap into the future. A violent release flings me onto my feet then, and I know that I have come out of it.

When I reached home I found a letter from Bergieri, asking unequivocally to see me when he gets back. That is still far off, at the beginning of October. There was an orchid from Martin, and a card from Augustin that I no longer expected. Its message was unremarkable, and its very niceness twisted my heart. He did not apologize for having left for America without phoning. But he calls me his youth, and that is enough to throw up the bridge of reminiscence between us. "Yours, my youth—Augustin." Those last four words mean a great deal to me. They mean everything.

I started a real cousin's letter to Augustin, too. But I could not stick to the part all the way through. I began to write very quickly, impetuously, and I did not read it over. On purpose. And although I do not remember the exact words I scrawled, I know that I told him the truth. To force him to answer, I reminded him that I should soon have to decide whether to go to South America, and that I was very uncertain. Finally I asked his advice. "I hope you will answer me as quickly as possible—it is vitally important," I added in postscript.

I had hardly mailed the letter when I regretted it. I had the very distinct impression of having made a stupid mistake. Augustin is so rational! It's so easy to be rational when you work all day long, and when each evening you go back to a cornucopia of three girls who call you father.

Martin will never know how strong my imagination is: strong enough to convince myself that his orchid came from Augustin.

Now I can measure the exhaustion I accumulated; for my baptismal trip I did three thousand kilometers. When I look at the map, and when I follow the route I drove, when I see this star-shaped country whose contours I traced almost exactly,

I grow dizzy—as though I had moved along the edge of a real star with no law of gravity to keep me from the abyss.

I am browner and thinner. But Marion congratulated me and gave me an even larger check than I had anticipated; she has already received several million francs' worth of orders.

I expect Irina in two weeks. I asked Madame Bouquet, who will soon change her profession, to come every morning while she still can, and I stay in bed till noon. Deep in my big bed, the last echoing tremors of the motor, the last trace of my nervous exhaustion, of my high fever smother quietly and die. There I sometimes find a fleeting state that is like happiness.

Since I have returned, rested and completely awakened, I am struck by the fragmentation of my life lately—by the atomization of my self in all directions. Four Cardinal Points Society, a tour of France for the Maison Rapp, perhaps South America soon. And a change of apartments to be considered.

But if I do go, ought I to hold on to an apartment in Paris? What then, leave without even keeping a *pied-à-terre?* No more earth under my feet—how apt a symbol! I have lost all security. I cannot get my bearings, I cannot recognize myself, my life is bursting apart. Once again I feel like a tree left standing alone on a storm-blasted hill.

Martin's letters grow sweeter, and I think of him as a threat. Poor inoffensive Martin! But he really does threaten what I hold most dear—my interior independence. If I do not leave for South America, after all, I know that I shall not be able to begin another winter like the one that just passed. If I do not marry Martin I will take Bergieri for a lover, without loving him. Coldly. Teeth clenched. The way we go into surgery.

I know that, too, with an intimate, sorrowing knowledge, resigned to it ahead of time.

I think of Joseph less and less: and I wonder again whether I am not a little monster. Sometimes it seems to me he has always been dead.

"We've got to have a serious talk about this Cordobal thing," Georges Höberlin said when I came to the ministry at his request.

It's curious to see him there, enthroned behind the desk that belonged to Talleyrand, to Villèle, to Vergennes, and so many others. As blasé as one may be, as cynical and as conscious of belonging to a third-rank nation—the white royal aura still floats among the walls, the faint echo of the imperial trumpets has not yet died away; and for a fleeting moment the glory of young republics seems still to live.

Minister—just as he had dreamed of being when he was eighteen. Exactly such. Is this what we mean by complete success? It is clear that Höberlin never doubts for a minute that I am dazzled by his power. And yet the only real power he has over me he already had when we were in school together: the power to make me ugly with a glance. A sharp glance that has not changed. The boil is still there, too, on the neck, hidden by the same adhesive patch. It does me no good to sit two yards away from Höberlin—his nose still scratches at my face. What does antipathy consist of? When I look at Georges, I am obliged to admit that between us there is a physical discord, a cellular discrepancy. Thus the antipathy is both unfair and insurmountable. This man, whose success I cannot bring myself to admire, has nonetheless achieved his ambitions better than any other of our schoolmates. And that woman opposite him (I) who (I am certain of it) is not a woman in his eyes —he is the only one who is helping her in a concrete, effective way. Yes, life is funny.

I said those last few words aloud.

"Incorrigible!" he exclaims as he always did. "She could philosophize while the guillotine fell on her. I was talking about Cordobal."

"I came here to talk about him. What kind of work exactly would I be doing?"

"Everything and nothing, as indicated by the title you'd have. Your role would be somewhere between secretary and interpreter, itinerant ambassadress and general factotum. You might just as likely have to arrange a reception in honor of the president of Uruguay as handle the return of an Italian overseer's corpse from Chile to Calabria; you might be translating technical articles from the local press on the work in progress, or choosing the jewel Cordobal wants to give to some Argentine lady. You know—public relations!"

"None of that sounds very hard, Georges."

"I give you loyal warning: harder than you think. Cordobal is not an easy employer; he is a master in every sense of the word. He could phone you in the middle of the night to ask you for some simple information; he never sleeps himself. He could send you into the jungle to smooth over some difficulty between the natives and the engineers on a project—with a sleeping bag for a hotel room. Since he is never tired himself, he doesn't believe other people can be. He might also ask you to sleep with him: whether you say yes or no, he will have forgotten it by the next day. On the other hand, if you make a professional mistake, he will never forget it; and if you don't

170

make any, and give him full satisfaction, he will arrange to keep you down there. The building program is discontinued for the next three years. I believe you'll spend six months in Brazil, six months in Argentina, and the rest of the time in Chile and elsewhere. Vacations will be scarce, and so will rest and comfort. Something of a pioneer's life...."

I listen to the beautiful names, the strange program. I already see that I shall learn nothing more from Georges. Whenever I ask him precise questions—on the financial arrangements, for instance—he retreats behind this Cordobal, of whom he speaks with respect as though he were some occult and omnipresent power. His very name has a mysterious sonority, although I could never say why. I know that Georges can be trusted in such circumstances, and, since Georges answers for him, so can Cordobal himself.

"For heaven's sake!" he cries, "doesn't she realize what I'm offering her? Two and a half years of travel through the southern hemisphere, the future, life! And all because she had the ridiculous idea to study Spanish instead of English! Frankly, Costa, don't you want to get out of your rut?"

He calls for a map of South America. (Finger on a button, and a steward who lacks only a wig to look like a court footman. "Here you are, Mr. Minister." Bravo, old George—an excellent effect.) The map comes alive under the irritating tap of his finger; the dream takes on sudden reality. Names of white cities one never visits, borders of countries one never knows the locations of—they flare into brightness. As if, deep in a black night, cities and borders were lighting up their footlights for me.

"Suppose I asked you to wire my acceptance to Monsieur Cordobal right now?"

"Why so quick? Why so categoric?"

I smile. "Because it is written, 'But let your communication be, Yea, yea; Nay, nay: for whatsoever is more than these cometh of evil.' And it is yes."

"No," he replies. "For exactly that reason, not yet. Just exactly because Costa bases her decisions on the Scriptures. You've got to think about it."

"But why?"

"I'll tell you." He winks an eye at me. "Champell will be here at the end of the month." I recall too late that this minister is a concierge as well, that he knows everyone and keeps up with all the gossip. "You see I understand the situation. Wait till you've seen him again—it will cost you nothing; I've promised to give Cordobal your answer by the beginning of October, and if it's in the affirmative, you'll leave on the first of November. So you see, there's no hurry."

"Martin has nothing to do with it," I say, annoyed.

"You never know," Georges answers.

He gives his superior laugh, his look of knowing everything. I did not know, myself, that Martin was coming at the end of September. Yes, life is strange.

"You should have taken my acceptance right away," I said as I rose.

"Possibly. But I want to play fair with you."

His eternal protective pity for me shows in his eyes. He walks me to the door, fingering his bandage. He hands me over to the steward. I feel very small behind the man, in those noble galleries. But I am a friend of the minister! Suddenly I tell myself that Georges has been very good to me, and that there is no one more generous than an enemy who thinks himself victorious.

172

But I regret not having given a definite answer. Almost another three weeks of uncertainty.

On Sunday I went to lunch at the home of Madame Poccarde, who is expecting a child. Madame Poccarde is Eliane. She lives with her husband in her father's apartment, at Villeneuve-Saint-Georges. She has changed so much that I almost do not recognize my timid little companion in this young woman with her lips newly swollen and pulpy, recalling the bruise of a kiss. Her husband is a classic redhead—a nice redhead: trumpet nose and an open face. But he is not as fine as Eliane.

I notice that all the books have disappeared from the shelf. A collection of matchboxes is there instead, running from an old, metal-worked box dated 1830 to a little Soviet one.

"It's Pierre's hobby," Eliane tells me. "I sold my books, but I wouldn't have had the time to read them anyway, would I?"

Her father is obviously impressed by Pierre Poccarde; he has already developed the sly glance, the cautious manner of those who feel themselves in a minority, and barely tolerated. He approaches me and tries to re-create a kind of complicity between us: "Your son is getting married, too, Madame Fontaine? My girl told me. You'll see how it ages a person. You'll see!"

It's true, good Lord—it's true! Jean-Christophe will be married on the twenty-fifth of September. I will certainly be a grandmother next year. It's curious—for the first time it occurs to me that if I married Martin Champell I could have a child, too. To be a mother once more before becoming a grandmother. Why not? For a few minutes I taste the most elementary desire there is, and the least rational one. My third child.

... The one that, they say, finishes off the transformation from the acid young girl, through the anemic young mother, into the full-blooming woman! Oh, how well Nature does things —she will not grant you her recompense until she has made sure of her own replenishment.

But a child—what a miracle! Never mind Nature! I remember the dark eyes of Jean-Christophe, of Virginie. In their night-blue depths I watched wonderment glow at the first sight of the world, as it has glowed since man began.... I never forgot the sorrow of having no other child. (Augustin had four girls.) I almost feel a rush of milk in me....

"South America will be marvelous," Eliane exclaims. "Oh, Madame Fontaine! How lucky you are! You'll write me? Say you'll write us all about it! And will you send matchboxes to Pierre?"

"But I'm not sure yet I'll go," I said.

"You've got to go, Madame Fontaine. You've got to. You're lucky enough to be free," she adds; "I haven't even got time to read the newspaper any more." And she glances coyly at her husband, who smiles complacently.

An ideal couple, the Poccardes. An almost improbable one —a *Marie-Claire* or *France* cover picture: the wife feminine as can be in a nylon apron, and the husband puffing at his manly pipe. Why do I feel this vague sadness then? Could it be jealousy of that gently swollen belly? No. I'm not jealous. I imagine it is a kind of sorrow at seeing how easily this young girl, with all her possibilities, with all the demands she made on herself, has become an entirely different woman. Because her husband "does not drink," and because she has plainly found happiness with him, she no longer thinks about men who do drink, or of the wives of alcoholics; she is no longer

174

interested in the general problems that once aroused her. She will never read again—not even the newspaper, as she had said, laughing.

It does no good to tell myself, "She is happy, and that's what counts. She is happy, and happiness excuses everything." I cannot rest at the thought of her. Does this mean it is inevitable that happy women lose interest in the march of the world? That the home is enough to absorb all their energy? When I was twenty years old and happy the same thing happened to me. . . . I would not remind Eliane that she had sworn to work for some anti-alcohol league. But if she is no longer happy one day—if sorrow knocked at her door—what would she have left? Women's greatest error has been their jealous barring of the door of their homes, closing in their happiness or their misfortune. And men's strength has been opening that door every day. . . . When I think of that strength, I think, too, of the effort it represents. The effort is itself a fracturing, a break that must be made anew each day.

"She should go, shouldn't she, Pierre?"

Her clear voice catches me on a naked nerve. No, it is not easy to leave, to cross the threshold. This break with my whole past lies before me, like a ditch to be crossed. A step that a man takes every day, a liberating step. . . .

Pierre Poccarde approves warmly. I cannot help thinking how easy it is to advise people to go away, as long as one is sure oneself of remaining under a familiar roof. Then I remember that they took no vacation this summer, that they have never been outside of France, and that they have very little chance of ever leaving Villeneuve-Saint-Georges. Once again I reflect that nothing can be shared.

I visited the Petroffs, too. Léon has recovered and I learn

that Paule is pregnant. She, too! At her age! I fight down the
same nervous laughter I had felt six months ago. No, I did not
laugh; after all, there is only a few years' difference between
us. Did I even feel the desire to laugh? (But the Lord replied
to Sarah: "Nay, but thou didst laugh.")

A folding couch has taken the place of Mademoiselle du
Haut-sur-Pas' iron bed. The walls and the mansarded ceiling
press even heavier now about the intimacy of this maid's room
—how will there be space for the baby? The layette on the
washbasin, the potty behind the screen? My perpetual flux
tosses me to the other side of the wave; I want to fly away
through a starry night to cities like glowing checkerboards.

"You don't look at all well," Paule told me gently. "Are
you sure you can take that climate? The strain and the food?
And the South Americans? I would hesitate, if I were you.
I'm telling you frankly, I would hesitate."

"As a matter of fact, I think I've decided to do it," I said.

"Two years," Paule says again. "Two and a half years!
What about your mother? and Jean-Christophe? and your
friends? Don't you think it will be hard for Sylvestre, pet?
Doesn't she look tired?"

Léon gives his opinion, which I did not ask. He is sweet;
but why do people always suppose they must give advice? I
know very well that I am growing older, and that I am going
to be a grandmother; but I also know that I can still leave for
South America, or have a child! Whatever I choose! A child,
America— What wealth there suddenly is in my life—what
new potentialities, what youth! In any case, I shall not go on
with this crippled existence. I do not want to be alone again
as I am this evening between Paule and her husband, who kept
me to dinner. Around the bridge table—we lack a fourth, dead

176

or alive. I never invited Paule either more than once a year; and she, too, was always the third person between my husband and me. I knew she enjoyed food; I would order a particularly fine dinner of Albine (these long-unused words sound like a dirge in my ears—was I the woman who ordered special dinners from her cook? in what world? when?). And I had the pleasant sense of having done my duty! The worst of it was that I had. Paule is doing hers, too, this evening by keeping me, by sharing the Camembert and the can of marrons with me. But there can be no true sharing. A single woman does not live on the life of the couples around her; she dies of it.

At the end of the dinner Paule began to talk about Alexandrine. She had learned more about her suicide.

The night before it the atheist nun had gone to a doctor in the neighborhood complaining of insomnia. He had been disturbed by her appearance—beautiful and over-made-up, her stare a little rigid—and had prescribed only a mild sedative. But Alexandrine wanted to be sure. She wanted two tubes of phenobarbitol for that same evening; and she set about getting them with a demonic perseverance and cleverness.

She asked her druggist for one, and he gave it to her with no hesitation. Then, her manner completely innocent, she went to several other pharmacies, each time asking for a tube. You must have a prescription, she was told in each. She implored them—"Give me two tablets, then, just enough for tonight. I'm going to the doctor tomorrow."

Finally one druggist softened to her nun-like smile. By evening she had her forty pills.

"People who kill themselves," Paule concluded in a professorial tone, "are always succumbing to a temporary mental imbalance. No one commits suicide if he is in full possession of his faculties."

"Are you so sure of that?" I asked. "Are you so sure? And besides, who among us is safe from one of those sudden absolute depressions?"

"Oh, it's a question of will power," Paule answered airily. "Only will power."

Léon is doing the dishes behind the screen—a perfect example of the domestication of man by his amazon. But unconsciously, sensuously, while she speaks, Paule is stroking her sides, broad as those of a gestating mare. In a few months a child will fill this room with the smell of wool and milk that is different from any other smell. . . . Yes, this time I am sure of it: this bitter saliva in my mouth is envy. And if I married Martin I, too, could . . .

I've decided this, at any rate: either I marry Martin or I leave for the opposite hemisphere. I refuse any longer to be a part of this sorry herd, of this butcher's penful of single women. I want to escape the Association of Christian Widows forever! I want to leave behind the grotesque program of lonely women: coming out at solitaire, a ham slice and yoghurt, psychotherapy if they're rich, mediums if they're not, and the breviary of the classified ads (matrimonials, apartments, and employment). I want to leave the pendulum flux of self-indulgent temptation and self-revulsion. I have, of course, agreed to Bergieri's appointment for the beginning of October, which I had at first intended to refuse. But I am ashamed beforehand. I am ashamed because I feel myself less and less capable of loving him. Whenever I think of him, a song I heard over the radio hums in my head: "Love without love is a fire set to a

Persian rug; it is spilt wine. . . ." Love without love. I should have written that song myself—those are the very words that came to my mind the night I kissed Bergieri without joy.

Jean-Christophe is married. Instead of going from Marseilles to see Mother in Corsica, I came directly back to Paris, because I am expecting Irina's telegram at any moment. I am impatient for her—I need her experience. I like success: there is a harmony, a gladness in it that fits the very rhythm of the world itself.

At least that is the feeling I had at my son's wedding. How beautiful are these stolen moments of time, these halts of fulfillment wrenched from the procession toward nothingness! I saw my own young love beside his young love; I saw them forming a small unsinkable island above a sea tumbling with the suddenly powerless threats of atomic war, of planetary death, of the Chinese invasion. Beauty on the faces, youth in the hands—they were unarmed and all-powerful.

I had not known (had they hidden it from me, or was it a new plan?) that after their wedding trip to Rome, Jean-Christophe and Nadine leave for Dakar, where they will spend eighteen months. I took the shock without flinching. But it was hard to kiss my son for the last time. He is so tall that his mouth touched my hair, and mine leaned against the artery in his neck. "My darling," I said to him. "My darling." And then I was quiet, for there was no more to say.

But I had still to smell that faint, lightly bitter aroma of grass in Nadine's kiss, planted four times on my cheeks in the provincial manner. When Jean-Christophe crushes that grass in his mouth, all the perfumes of Araby— But I have learned to transpose my pain and Jean-Christophe's joy, and to measure his closeness to Nadine by the very distance I feel him from me. I want to feel that the loss of him is something I own.

I shall have no further reason for refusing to go to South America, since Jean-Christophe will be leaving for Dakar. I am sorry that Höberlin would not immediately accept the commitment I had been willing to make. I should like to feel that my going was all settled. I should like to take advantage of my desire to go, now that I have lost my son, after I have lost Augustin. I can have no illusions: Nadine is from the south, Jean-Christophe is interested in Africa—they may never come back to France, not even to Marseilles. I prepare to leave, too, as though I were certain of it. Renew my passport. Look for a furniture storage house. Talk to the landlord. Everything incites me to separation. The tiny clustered fibers of my life come apart, one by one. The hard pit of my security has melted, and I feel more and more free. Fantastically, each of my bonds is giving, one after another. Even this apartment which I could not keep even if I were to remain in Paris, because the new taxes would ruin me. Even Madame Bouquet, who has left me at last for good. She has bought an old Peugeot; I imagine I will meet her someday, twisting her wheel like the wheel of fortune, beckoning me into her taxi with a proprietary gesture. Even Irina, who is postponing her visit again (again, Irina!). "Wieland has asked me to start my European trip in Munich—how can I refuse? So I have changed my booking. But if you'll still have me, I'd like to make a round trip to Paris from Munich next month. I can't tell you the exact date yet: it will depend on Wieland's plans . . ."

Wieland! Wieland! I feel that she no longer belongs to herself, and no longer belongs to me. Wieland is the one who counts for her, who will always be first from now on. Our roles are reversed.

Since I became a widow I have seen how incomplete my friendship for her had grown. So many times in ten years she had written "Why don't you come to Canada? I can get you a reduced plane fare, and I have a big *vivoir* and two beds here." But I, knowing that my husband would refuse me the two or three hundred thousand francs I would need for the trip, and not daring to confess it to Irina, would retreat behind my conjugal obligations. And when I went to Chicago, I did not even manage to make a quick trip to Montreal! On my return, I wrote her that I had been obliged to go everywhere with my husband. Had she suffered at feeling me so distant, too? Because at bottom Irina may be like all women. Irina— Irina, too.

Höberlin was right. Martin Champell is in France for a week, in Paris and in Lacq. For a moment I was tempted—but I quickly brushed the urge aside—to handle Martin skillfully, to make him wait out the two and a half years my absence would last. After all, he never has married; the chronically enamored are as incurable as arthritics. But I am incapable of guile. I must decide: yes or no, once and for all. Whatsoever is more than these . . .

I may as well admit it. Decided as I might be to give Martin up, it hurts me to think it will be for good. From the moment he arrived, I felt as though I were setting a bundle into his round hands; that I was unburdened of all responsibility, and even of myself. He had no sooner appeared than he scolded me gently: "How tired you look, my dear! You were mad to make such a trip this summer. It was much too hard for a little woman like you." (In Martin's eyes I am a fragile blonde.) "And now no cleaning woman? You will do me the favor of finding yourself another one tomorrow. Otherwise I will not come to lunch. I hope at least you're not still thinking of South America."

"Actually, there is still some question of it."

"But I forbid it! I know Cordobal's reputation. A genius, perhaps. But a first-class exploiter—he'll kill you with work! How much is he offering you?"

"I—Höberlin doesn't know."

"Naturally not. Cordobal manages with his charm, and the worst thing about it is that it works for him! People would drudge for him for nothing. Suppose you wanted to come back and he wouldn't give you the money for it?"

"I'd wash dishes on a freighter!"

"I'm talking seriously, my dear. And what about your apartment?"

"I would cancel my lease, if I went," I replied. "And store my furniture."

"And you'll never come back." His tone is so categorical that I feel uneasy. He is right, after all; I am trusting too heavily to Höberlin. Suddenly I am a little afraid of Cordobal. "You will never come back . . ."

"You must not go," Martin finishes, his tone positive.

"You think not?"

"I have forbidden it, Sylvestre!"

Where did he get that self-assurance? It is as though he were certain of having won already. He speaks to me as a master—as a loving master, the tone that women like best. A tacit agreement forms between us: he comes every other day to lunch at my apartment. Each evening we dine together at the Crillon.

I subject Martin to objective examination. After all, I should know exactly what I am giving up; I should measure the dimensions of the sacrifice I am making to myself. I want to be sure that ultimately it is a limited one. Here is a man I could marry; I certainly have the right to weigh him, to stand him up to the yardstick and measure myself against him. Let's see.

A little shorter than I. And much fatter. Eyes about which I have nothing to say. Physically, he neither repels nor attracts me: he is. He is he. I am I. Women with great experience claim that one can get used to any man. Martin is ugly, but he is athletic and healthy. His stay in the desert lends him something of the flair of the adventurer he is not. His mind is more open than I had thought. When he has exhausted oil and I have avoided ethnography, he shows interest in everything I talk about. In my friends, my reading, Jean-Christophe. And even in Irina. He is clever, yet at the same time there is that boyish, good-egg kindness which is at once amiable and irritating. His tone detached, he asks whether I have heard from "Monsieur Costa." Belligerently I snap "A postcard!" At first he is silent; then, like a good sport, he offers an excuse: "Big cities really devour a person's time. They're such immense organisms. . . ."

There are, of course, many subjects we do not agree on. But I am so accustomed to keeping my own counsel, from the past, that I have no trouble avoiding the touchy subjects by absolutely infallible reflex. But each time we touch on a dangerous topic, I watch Martin. I watch him with such intensity that it seems as though I have a thousand eyes, all of them burning. And I sense once again what a terrible thing it is to

183

set two human beings face to face forever, two humans each with a heart, a brain, his own tastes; each with a skin and a smell. Even when they love one another it is hard. But when they do not! Where do I get the idea that the couple is the only natural unit? Is that one of the traps nature sets? But I am not interested in helping the species to multiply. It gets along fine all by itself. When I long for a child by Martin, it is not for the sake of the species, nor is it to ensure the continuation of the Champell name.

It is because I want to possess a small god all to myself.

I followed Martin's advice. I went to the employment bureau to ask for a housekeeper.

There in that hideous office, conceived according to the norms of another age, I grew aware once again of the equivocal character of all those people whom I call intermediaries. A case in point: the directress of the agency, who shares both in the proletarian condition and in the respectability of the employer.

Between the well-dressed woman (me) who is offering a position and the bareheaded woman seeking one—between the supply and the demand—stands the intermediary. Why is the role ambiguous? Because the intermediary must lie to both parties, and give each of them the impression that she is on his side, in collusion with him against the other; meanwhile, paradoxically, each party has the impression that it is himself who is being told lies.

Double agent in the very conception; traitor by definition. The falsest position there is, and loathsome, too—loathsome above all—because it is necessary, and because it forces an awareness of the chasm that separates certain sectors of humanity from others.

On my way home (I had hired a Spanish woman solely on the recommendation of the agency directress) I considered that everyone who has the power to put us in contact with another world—the clairvoyant, the sorcerer, the procurer, the abortionist—has the same unpleasant aura, because they cause us to feel the ambiguity or the injustice of a situation, or the premonition of its danger. But how can we do without the intermediary? When I interpret for Cordobal's company, I shall be a kind of intermediary, too. I shall try to be a—a mediator, instead.

The word "mediator" made me think again. Suddenly it occurred to me that at the other end of the ladder, way up on top, there was an intermediary, too, the total Mediator, the Priest for eternity, and that the most sordid of situations are still only the demonic reverse images of Truth.

So that I was not wrong in feeling that my husband was a barrier and a mediator at the same time. Perhaps it is impossible to live without an intermediary? Perhaps it is excessive pride to think it possible to do without one?

I should have remembered that Höberlin has only a kind of genius, but he has it at its highest degree of perfection: that of sensing his adversary's weak point, which is unknown even to that person. When I phoned him about Cordobal, he snickered, "Champell has obviously been at work!"

"Yes, but you've got to admit you've left him plenty of room. I know almost nothing about Monsieur Cordobal, and nothing at all about my salary."

"Is it to Martin Champell's advantage that you stay here?

Yes. Is it to mine that you go? No. Why don't you trust me then when I tell you that Cordobal is a decent, honest man and a great man?"

"But—"

"But Sylvestre Costa is already feeling less eager about going," he murmured. "Which is what I expected. I'm not saying I blame you, you know."

And he hung up.

One point for you, old George! It's true that I am less eager to go. An insidious temptation is softening me, weakening me, decomposing me. I drowse in the torpor that comes before anesthesia.

Augustin's orchid is dead, but I live among tall roses—I who used to live on anemones. Once again my bones, accustomed to my little two-cylinder car, have come to know the gentleness of the Citroën's springs; after the garlic reek in the truck drivers' restaurants I smell the aroma of delicate sauces in elegant dining rooms! But I have no fear of dozing into the waking dream of the rich. No—I constantly forget that Martin is a rich man. All I want now is the necessities, and that is what is most dangerous. Because it is the necessities that Martin would bring me.

Frankly, I feel good with him. Yes, that is what is most dangerous. I am no longer bored when I am with him—he listens to me so willingly! I have found my brother again. A brother in love: what a dream! But alas, an innocent dream; with Martin I feel in mortal safety. What disturbs me, what is turning my head, is not simple desire. It is the far more elemental and far crueller desire to have a roof, a man, a child.

To come to pleasure through Augustin—yes, that would be like entering the body of the sun. . . .

When Martin told me he would be returning to Paris for good in six months, and that he was going to buy an apartment, he watched carefully for my reaction. But how could he reckon the effect of those few words, spoken with the embarrassment of the very simple man he basically is—"I'm looking for a modern five rooms, with a terrace, and a view of the Bois."

Only very lonely and very poor women can understand this: it is not necessarily shameful to be tempted by a terrace on the ninth floor of a white house—a terrace where a child learns to walk in the sun. . . . It is not necessarily shameful to miss an apartment where one has lived for twenty-five years; to want another home, a floor to put one's furniture on piece by piece, lovingly, and arrange them like flowers, and walk among them as in a forest. Furniture, wood cut down, replanted trees, a winter garden. . . .

Or perhaps it would be those very women—the loneliest, the poorest—who would think me wrong, and the rich or happy ones right, because the latter attach a value to their well-being that the less privileged women have trained themselves to scorn? I do not know; I can no longer tell.

I wrote Irina to ask her advice. I like advice from her, just because she hates to give it. She yields her opinion only with distaste, but I have always thought that extorted counsel is the only kind worth while. What sort of value can there be to advice that is scattered cheaply about by the handful? Irina's drops like rare pearls, long ripened in the fold of a shell.

Despite what Joseph may have supposed, it was she who

persuaded me that I would be wrong to leave him, when Virginie died and I wanted briefly to go, anywhere, to forget. . . .

The night before he leaves for Lacq, Martin finally speaks to me. My radio has been working badly and since he loves to putter, he offered to fix it for me. From his seat on the floor amid bolts and tubes he asks me suddenly, with the roughness of very timid people: "Why don't you marry me, my dear? You know I love you."

Oh, the wiles I have learned since I am a widow—I who never lied! My surprise seems sincere. Coquettishly, I pretend astonishment. Actually I know that the immediacy of the decision terrifies me, and I am only trying to gain time. Just a little more time, Martin! Just time enough to receive (a letter from Augustin) Irina's answer. But that is cowardly, Sylvestre; cowardly. You already know that Augustin will not write and that Irina will give you no advice. You must choose. You must make your choice alone.

"Good Lord," I finally say. "You've taken me by surprise!" (That's true: I feel as startled as though I had never even asked myself the question!) "I haven't got my balance yet." (But that is false. Pardon me, Jo; pardon me!) "It's so touching, I don't know how to—"

"You didn't say no!" Martin cried, bounding to his feet.

The simplicity of his excitement and his guilelessness disarm me. "Of course I didn't say no!"

"Then it's yes?"

He dances from one foot to the other. His surprise, his joy touch me. I feel beautiful, young, all-powerful. Might he, too, have the power to re-create me, simply because his glance is another's, and only others give us life? His eyes watch me—those eyes I cannot describe except that they see, they look.

188

(Augustin's eyes have no color either, but it is because their light is light before any refraction; it is the prism reassembled.) I thrust away the memory, the eyes, the name with rage. Augustin did not answer me. He will never answer me.

"It's such a serious thing, Martin! We're not twenty years old any more. Can't we think about it—a little?"

"I've already thought about it."

"And wait a little while yet?"

The perilous word is said; I am relieved. "Wait." What will he say? He sits beside me, he takes my hand. I notice only that his nails are well tended. Yes, that is all I feel when he touches me: the hygienic pleasure of knowing him to be so clean. The tonic, cold pleasure you feel in a handsome bathroom.

"It's true that we're not twenty any more," he says. "That's just the reason we can't wait too long—"

"I didn't say for long!"

But truthfully, I had thought it; my dream—my cowardly, cynical dream—is probably to lose nothing, to reconcile everything, to leave for South America keeping this good heart in reserve, keeping this faithful dog on the leash. Look, that's impossible! I know very well it's impossible. If I did not know it, Martin would deprive me of my last hope. "I like things to be clear," he says. "I won't go back to the Sahara for six months without knowing what you're going to do with me."

"But you're leaving for Lacq tomorrow, aren't you?"

"And coming back to Paris next week, yes. Listen. I'll be gone for three or four days. Only tell me I can think of you in a special way during those few days."

I do not know who answered—it was not I, it was my voice. Or my weakness, or my fondness, or a still deeper instinct. But I heard my voice: "Yes, Martin."

189

And his lips, which are not lips to me, kiss my palms long and humbly.

As he was leaving he stopped abruptly, pointing his finger at that weekly paper lying on the table. "You read *that?*"

I felt vaguely disturbed, obscurely guilty, in a way I had forgotten. Then I hardened, as I used to. I answered yes. It was not Martin alone I was answering. It's curious—a word, a single word, can betray a man, and reveal his system of thought; but it can evoke a whole world, too, through immediate associations. "That" was the word Great-uncle Fontaine always used at Neuves for whatever was not his race, his group, his opinions, to such an extent that he applied the neuter to individuals as well as to objects. I can still hear him remarking on the pretty storekeeper at Neuves—"My word, *that* certainly dresses to kill!"

Martin had kept his finger outstretched a few inches from the paper, with the disgusted air of someone afraid of catching a germ from its touch. Then he dropped it. "Not I. Never. It smells of Jews."

"Why? Do they have an odor?"

It fell spontaneously from my mouth, before any thought. Martin looked at me, perplexed. I began to laugh. "You know, sometimes I think I'd like to found a pro-Semitic party!"

"Is this some kind of mania in the Costa family, founding parties? What happened to the French labor party?"

This outright allusion to Augustin clipped my breath at first. Then I remembered that this was to be my lot, from now on, in any case: I should have to speak easily of him, and think tranquilly of him. I contrived to laugh again.

"It may be a mania—Mother is founding Associations of Christian Widows all over Corsica at this very moment!"

But Martin does not even smile. Instead, he gazes at me with immense gravity. "I like that element of the fantastic in you," he said finally. "I've always thought you were a poet...."

"A poet?" I answered, stunned. "Not at all." I was laughing no longer now; there was a reproach in his voice—or was it irony? "I have an open mind, that's all. That paper is only one detail; I read a great many papers, that one among others. What is important, Martin, is that I have certain opinions and ideas I believe in, because I have developed them over a long while."

"But so have I," Martin said gently. "I've already told you I was conservative, and I fully intend to die a reactionary. You can see I'm not afraid of words. I consider democracy as it is practiced in this country to be the greatest enemy of the people."

"Perhaps it is." I flared with sudden passion. "But it is an enemy worthy of them!"

Augustin's phrase had just crossed my mind: that liberty was more important even than justice. "Martin, you're a good Catholic, aren't you." (This was not even a question.) "Well, according to the strictest orthodoxy, God knew the enormous amount of evil and suffering that would derive from man's liberty, and yet He chose to assume that truly inhuman responsibility—and create free man."

"Which means?"

"That any evil is preferable to the absence of freedom. Perhaps even injustice."

"That argument can go a long way."

"As far as possible! Listen, I never told you this before, but you've got to know it: there is nothing I set higher than the search for truth; I would suffer from nothing more than not being able to speak my own convictions, discuss my own opinions. I've always known that you don't share them all. But could we speak simply and calmly about them, and discuss them like two friends?"

"No," Martin says, with that gentleness that reminds me of something else (but what?). "Discussions always turn into arguments. And it's so futile! Do you think I could change my attitudes at my age? I'm over fifty. And I have no desire to change. And I don't ask you to change; you have the right to stay what you are, my dear: a delightful revolutionary."

"Fine."

That is all I say—"Fine." But deep inside me a small scarred wound has reopened. So old, so forgotten—and suddenly so bloody and so present that I am scarcely surprised. Just as if I had learned that the lung lesion I had contracted in childhood had gone on, unknown to me; and now it was clear that it had spread, it corrodes my whole lung, it sends me back to the same bed, the same doctor, the same asphyxiation. . . .

Martin is watching me as intently as he can. The contrast between that bulging eye, almost globular now, and the indulgence in the voice that had called me a poet—the contrast makes me ill at ease. In those round eyes I read that I am being judged.

Yes—yes, Martin is judging me! He must be thinking that I am an idealist, but that I am not dangerous. When did I hear those words before? Martin is judging me, but fundamentally the verdict does not matter to him. Do a woman's opinions count, after all? How sweet to see a woman talking politics; it's amusing, it's so incongruous, says the tone of voice. Whereas

192

I, Martin, because I am a man, I hold my opinions by divine right. That is what the eyes are saying.

I know it now. Perhaps I had always known it. That gentleness that sets its power of inertia against my urgency—it is the gentleness of the meek who possess the earth (but not the heavens). The glance I could not define is a glance I know well, and yet I have only just now recognized it. It is the tiny pebble deep in the eyes, that hard stone that nothing could crumble, over which the ocean might roll without leaving a mark; it is the opaque glance of fish; it is Jos—

And I say nothing at all! And I make not a move! All at once I have taken up the old habit I had when my husband was alive, of playing dead when he turned that eye on me. What good does it do to speak? What can I say? Martin is right, all discussions turn into arguments. I must let him go ... wait till he returns ... I still have a few days of grace. A few days. I notice the unmistakable mark of a bachelor life, the tiny end of a cleaner's tag sticking out beyond the handsome sleeve. I cannot restrain my hand: I remove it carefully. Then I say as kindly as I can, "Good-by, Martin. Have a good stay in Lacq."

He seems reassured by my automatic gesture, by the banally feminine reflex. He kisses the palms of my hands.

"Good-by, my little poet. Thank you."

How can it be? Who am I? What have I become? What am I ready to become once again? I must admit it—not even that discovery was enough to turn me from Martin. It almost seems to me that this sudden likeness between Joseph and Martin is—should I call it a sign? A sad sign. The symbol of my fate, which might be never to fulfill myself? The slope slants gentler and gentler, easier and easier.... Doesn't that

193

prove that the weakest part of me, or the simplest and the most concrete part, needs the very environment I thought was stifling me? I smothered there, but after all I did live in it. Poet. That is what Martin will call me. Jo called me "silly." It is the same thing. There were nights this past winter when I would have given anything to hear myself called "silly little woman."

My beliefs are important to me, of course, and so is my freedom of thought. I even thought they were tremendously important. But to defend them, I need to be sure that someone needs me to do so. (As Augustin would need it.) A woman of my age, without professional experience, without contact in other circles than her own—what can she do? I may be the last bourgeoise, the last woman to embody a damned generation. But I am that woman, and I can do nothing about it. Can you say as much, Augustin? Besides, I am probably not the only one, nor the last such woman. Europe is full of single women, forty or fifty years old, obsessed by the fear of growing old, broken by the mold of their class or their habits; Europe is full of widows, Europe is full of dead women. There are ten million too many women in Europe. Ten million. The entire population of Belgium, or of New York. And in the world, I think, there are forty-five million too many women. A whole France-full of women. . . .

So, when one of them finds a way to stop being extra, when someone is willing to grant her a small place, doesn't it seem extremely prideful to refuse that place?

No! No, not so much prideful as strong. It takes a lot of strength to carry oneself. . . . There are forty-five million women whom no one taught to carry themselves. Those who claim the contrary are lying. Each of us must come to know

from her own lips the taste of loneliness and the taste of freedom, as mingled as water and salt in those mouthfuls of ocean
one swallows, that are cool and bitter at once....

What I must know is whether, for me, it is not too late.

That is what Augustin said, too—"It is too late." And I know
now that when he said it, drawing his finger through my hair,
he was not thinking only of his youth's ideals; he meant, too,
a possible closeness between us—which he wanted to make impossible. His tone was the tone of a man who has renounced
everything.

Occasionally the insane idea occurs to me to write him again,
to tell him about Martin, to ask his advice again. But I know
I will not do it. A sad instinct tells me that he might answer,
"Marry Monsieur Champell, my little Sylvestre—marry!" As
Irina, another time, advised me to stay with my husband.

It's not good to need so much time to think before making
a decision. Where there is no love, reflection begins. Where
there is no love, the reign of intellect begins. Where there is no
love, there is the wily, complicated, stupid intellect. Where
there is no love, there is death.

The days pass. The hours. Sometimes I want to open my
windows, and call to the women walking, marketing, airing
the dog or the baby. I want to cry, "What would you do in
my place? In a way, my life depends on the answer I must
give in a few days from now."

In three days.

Two.

Tomorrow.

Tomorrow Höberlin is expecting my answer. And Martin returns the day after tomorrow.

What would they do in my place? Oh, it would be good to call to them, to ask them my question, and to see them as confused as I. I imagine their opinions would be as divided as my own. No—I'm very much afraid they would not be. . . . I wonder if the great majority of women, in my place, would not throw themselves on Martin like dogs on a bone, like plague victims toward a well. Because he loves me, because I am fond of him, and because I am going to be forty-five. The brief but intense experience I have had of the life of single women has taught me what degree of weakness strong women can reach. There are no amazons in this age of female emancipation.

Even among the others, how few there would be—what an infinitesimal minority—who would advise me to leave the prey for the shadow, to give up a sensible marriage and total security! I think of Mother; Annie; Paule; Eliane; Marion; Madame Bouquet; and the bizarre idea occurs to me that Claude Bergieri would perhaps be the only one to tell me not to marry Martin. Perhaps Nadine, too, paradoxically. Nadine is so young that she cannot accept even the idea of growing old, of renunciation, of no longer loving. "I shall always be young, I will never grow old," she likes to say. But under her laughter there is rage, there is a desperate effort to conjure fate, to nullify death. One day she looked at me and seemed to see my face for the first time.

"You've stayed very young," she told me; and, pointing to Jean-Christophe, "You don't look as though you could be his mother at all—it's true." I realized in a brief flash that she could be jealous of me; but that besides, and to the same extent, I was the incarnation of her hope. She would watch herself grow old in me, as eternally young as Jean-Christophe sees me.

I expect a letter from Irina with each mail delivery. But I begin to fear that her answer will be no help to me. I am alone, entirely alone with the choice. Alone between the child I could still bear and the continent I could still discover! A child or America—equivalent weights. A child is certainly worth a continent. But the child implies Martin: around a child there must be a father, a family, a home. Actually, I must decide, and decide by myself, what I am. A woman saturated with herself by eighteen months of solitude, choosing freely to move out of herself one last time into a maternity that would be a late-day one and that much the happier; or else a woman capable of fulfilling herself through work external to herself, capable of responsibility for herself, and preferring a difficult independence to a marriage of reason.

Martin. . . . I need only phone him, or write him, in Lacq. I need say only a word—the great "yes" of a telegram, the "yes" of an election ballot—and I am a wife once again. Madame Champell this time. What does it matter, since I was able neither to remain Sylvestre Costa nor to become her again? Yes, at the moment of taking a third name it seems to me perhaps unjust that a woman should completely lose her first. But since no woman protests, why should I stand out against it? I haven't the suffragette soul any more. Before the war, how many women were seriously troubled at not having the right to vote, while I felt it a searing humiliation? Once married, I never thought of it again. Perhaps one can get used to anything. Sometimes I imagine Augustin at the U.N.; I am sure that he is often obliged to keep silent, champing at his bit, when he wants to shout back at a lie. I still hear him: "Diplo-macy is a method of bringing myself into line." A marriage of reason is the way women have of bringing themselves into line. Perhaps in the end we are all, men and women both, fed up with the little aborted eggs of our ambitions and our hopes, rotting slowly inside us, right up to the final infection and decomposition.

Martin. . . . I will be the adventuress returned to legality, the aging actress who agrees to play the role she had once re-fused in the flare of youth. The disappointed woman of ambi-tion who finds a certain pleasure in denying herself.

Martin. . . . All my powers will drowse into sleep. My body's sensuality, my mind's disquiet will rest in his arms, uncured, unsoothed, unsaved. Anesthetized. Drugged. And I will only awaken again on the day of my death.

Martin. . . . I will sleep—oh, how I shall sleep! I will slide swiftly into the element I love best—sleep. Actually, many people spend their lives asleep, and do not know it. I, at least, I shall be deliciously aware of the fact. "There are seven hun-dred million Chinese?" I shall ask, yawning and stretching. "Who cares? I'm sleeping. They're hungry? They should go to sleep—'he who sleeps forgets his hunger' . . ." And the morn-ing of the last day of the world, the last chambermaid in the world will bring me my last breakfast in bed, with Marie Antoinette's last brioche, at the sound of the last trumpet!

Martin. . . . It will all be over—reading the classified ads, worrying about my apartment, riding in a little car along the perilous borders of a star, asking Georges Höberlin for help, sending my picture to other Cordobals, dreading menopause, burning alone in my wide bed. The idealists will say I am wrong, of course; but there are so few of them that virtually everyone will tell me I am right, with the secret satisfaction of seeing me become like all the rest of the world again. They will recognize a certain mark on Martin's brotherly head, and they will feel a strange reassurance. And perhaps they will be right: a marriage of reason has as much chance of success as the love marriage I thought I was entering at twenty. I expected everything from my poor Jo; I was the one who was wrong. I expect nothing of Martin that he cannot give me—his presence, security, the precious routine of physical exchange. And the child—that continent—

Martin. . . . I shall have a little girl. She will be dark like me, with her father's good cheeks. Or a little boy who will give me back Jean-Christophe's baby smell. . . .

On the other hand—oh, on the other hand!—lies the unknown. Adventure, Höberlin called it. It is much more for me; it is the fracture, the break. The freely-assumed gamble of starting a new life at the age when all things finish. It is the parachutist's jump, the gull's swoop, the search for the Grail and for the white whale. It is the first stage of a separation for which everything has mysteriously prepared me. It is a kind of active retreat, which I enter to survey my strength, and to gird myself toward some end I cannot yet foresee.

To the warehouse, you things I have loved so well—my round table, my gondola chairs, the marriage bed, my swan's-neck couch. Farewell, things too often seen, faces too familiar, books too much read, opportunities lost! I drop the prey for the shadow, and despite what prudence and good sense dictate, that is what must be done. For he who would save his life will lose it. The prey is measurable matter; it is the apparent and the weighty. The shadow is the invisible and the spirit; the shadow is grace. To leap, feet joined, into the void like the parachutist and like the suicide—what dazzlement, how far beyond anguish!

Oh, huge liberty! desolate freedom! An endless succession of hotel rooms, valises forever shut and opened; eternal departure, eternal return! Liberty—gray or splendoring dawns, bright-lit evenings or frozen nights! Liberty—faces forever new, landscapes springing forever new under my eyes, golden cities, earthen villages, a new continent!

Oh, liberty—hard liberty! I go without farewell, ten thousand kilometers from my land and my son. Pressed toward the void by the millions of younger women who each year rise from their sea of childhood like so many small Venuses Anadyomene, and gape open the same avid mouth as Nadine—thrust toward the void, I protest with all my pitiable strength. I resist their relentless pressure, I proclaim my right to go on living, my right to hope with all hope that one day on the immense sea of freedom my wandering boat will meet the thousand-bannered ship of the one man who could set fire to my life, could set it burning with the fire of his eyes and his smile.

That, too, is madness. . . . But is it? To go to South America because Augustin Costa lives in New York. Is that really so wild a delusion? I need only go, and everything becomes possible. Because as soon as one starts flying around the world, the world shrinks to the size of an orange—that fruit of the sun, that red ball we can toss in our hand. (I remember the one thing Irina ever confided about her meetings with Wieland—meetings that became the theme of my sterile musings. The best was at Vancouver: she had crossed Canada to meet him for a weekend, and he came from Japan for her!)

It seems to me that the difference we feel between Europeans and Americans arises from the fact that all Americans are the descendants—at one, two, or ten generations' remove—of men who had the courage to wrench their feet from the soil of an old country, to shake the dust from their soles, and to cross an ocean. The main thing is to unstick oneself from the soil a first time. Once we begin to fly about the globe, we are saved. Saved by everything we have agreed to lose. . . . Then, because we no longer belong entirely to the earth, we can dream of gathering one by one a necklace of stars.

Nevertheless, I will not disavow myself. Neither myself nor my country. Nor—no, not even my class, now. I will go into death with all my weapons, as Augustin says. What are my weapons? First, I think, a despairing humility under my apparent pride—a sad humility that retains me from believing that my story presents any personal interest to the eyes of God. (I am the comma, the dash, or the space in an isolated line amid the numberless pages of a book that is still being written each day.) Then, I think, a nearly complete interior freedom—such a freedom that sometimes I even question that truth that seems to me the only one we can be sure of: that our God is the god of the whole universe. Might He not be the almost local god, so to speak, of our own solar system? Or the Spirit of our own planet, perhaps? Or only an emanation of ourselves? Perhaps we created God by dying.

And then, above all, I think my greatest weapon is that nearly infinite resistance to frustration, which I inherit from the generations before me. Resistance to frustration, which is quite different from self-repression. I do not repress my desires: they show clearer on my face than the lines do—and I bear the familiar unfulfillment before me in the hollow cup of my hands.

No, I am no longer young enough or strong enough to deny this milieu that has shaped me and whose stigmata mark me down to my very bones. I know that even in the hottest climes I shall keep my cold little smile, my good-child manner. It is probable that if Cordobal offers me the symbolic glass of water I will draw back from it just as I do from Bergieri—my aversion grows each day that brings our appointment closer. No, I will never swallow love like a glass of water—I would rather grow thirsty. And in any case I have only to wait a few more years and no one will offer me anything at all.

What does it matter?

I want all or nothing. Love or no one. There is where all my madness lies.

I shall survey Europe from a great distance; to see what's left of it, what it looks like seen from the other side of the equator with my head wrong side up and the polar icecap upside down. Perhaps its little faraway splendors will appear as the jewels of a mummy queen, or the gleams of a rising star. Or like Achilles' shield, where the whole civilization of the Greek islands is chiseled. Perhaps it will seem to be the world's one standard, the only land to achieve human scale.

I consider which ten or twelve books I will take with me, as if to a hypothetical desert island. The choice shrinks—first it is like puckered leather, then a burned house with only the girders left; then a single beam; then the cornerstone. What shall I take? Corneille would be grotesque, Balzac old-fashioned, Chateaubriand and Proust too painful because of Combourg and Combray (I can allow no nostalgia). The Bible and the *Upanishads*, of course. The *Divine Comedy* and the *Gitanjali*. Pascal, Nietzsche, and *The Brothers Karamazov*.

A Faulkner novel and a Graham Greene—which, I don't know yet. Molière *or* La Fontaine. Bernanos *or* Claudel.

Plus three or four books I prize, for personal reasons or for no reason at all. Which, quite simply, I love.

To be honest with myself, I must acknowledge that nothing truly interests me but the eternal destiny in store for us: eternal consciousness or eternal sleep.

Yes, I believe that the greatest war of all time—and it scorns to take place in any but a few tormented spirits—is the pacific war between the two religious systems that divide the world. The difference is not so much at the level of the individual, who is sacrificed in either case, as at the level of God Himself. From the Law to the gospels, the Bible has given the West the hope or the certainty of a conscious, personal God, who numbers our days, our hairs, our sins; and who gathers us up on the day of our death, to raise us to his face. But the other half of the world limits itself to desiring eternal sleep—which I often fear (or hope) is our only end.

No, nothing is more important than that war; neither my life, nor the atomic war, nor cancer—no earthly or partial death. Between two immensities so vast that the notions of time and space are meaningless in them we live for the duration of a lightning flash. How does that flash achieve such intensity in its briefness? Nothing is more intense, more painful, more ephemeral than our consciousness of living. How can we do other than aspire to death? I think that sometimes I begin—oh, not to desire death. Not yet. But to have no more fear of dying.

I believe, too, that I finally understand why all religions have preached renunciation and chastity. It is not because the pleasures of this world, and love, are bad; it is precisely because they are good that they must be renounced. Because the truth of life, and its only absolute, is death; and whatever attaches us to the world—and attaches us mainly by what is good and desirable in it—delays our necessary, our unavoidable separation from it. . . . If I had been given the supreme gift, Augustin, life would have seemed to me such a perfect whole, so sufficient a god, so necessary a good, that I might not have sought to prolong it. I would have curled in a ball at the feet of that man, as an animal lies down and curls at the feet of its master.

One moment more.
And death would have come . . .
But a naked hand
Came then . . .

For me, the hand has been withdrawn. The "moment more" is over. Now it is time for death.

I should have expected it. Irina will not come. She and Wieland have been married, almost secretly, in some faraway corner of Bavaria. They are going to Sicily where Wieland will write a life of Wagner, and they will not come back to Munich till Christmas.

Among the pages of her long letter she slipped a snapshot of her wedding—the only picture there is of it. Before the steps of a small baroque church, whose bell tower ends in a gilded onion dome, stand a heavy man with white curls and a woman in a suit. I scarcely recognize her. Irina's indestructible Finnish beauty, which derives from the rhythmic strength of the bone structure, is hidden by the too-heavy dark suit.

The pearl of her face disappears beneath a flowered hat. The gloved hands grasp a round bouquet. Can it be? This solid German wife beside an elderly musician—can this be Irina? Is this all the poetry, all the love, the eternal youngness of the world—this woman? This timid, proud bride's smile—is this the expression of the being who was all the sensuality, all the passion in the world? This woman grown thick, and badly dressed—is this the sea bird and the helicopter, the *Lotta* of 1939 and last year's air hostess? Yes, Sylvestre, this is Irina. It is Irina at forty. It is Irina happy.

I knew beforehand that she would give me no advice, that she would stand behind the fact that she does not know Martin Champell. But in her letter there is something I did not expect: she gives of herself more than I have ever known her to do during twenty years of friendship. I know what that means. I remember what she told me when she passed through Paris in 1944, with her husband. I did not know that Clarke had reached the last stages of addiction; I found it out by chance. We were lunching together, she and I, in an American club, when Irina was approached by a tall girl; her eyes were heavy with drug and her body was thin as the victim of a concentration camp. She was a French girl whom Irina had known in London; with absolute simplicity Irina talked to her about Clarke's vice and the cure he was going to attempt back in the United States. My astonishment must have been evident, for scarcely had the girl turned away than Irina smiled sadly.

"Yes, it's true," she said. "But I had no reason to tell you about it; whereas it could help that human relic, or at least give her some hope. When there's nothing more you can do for your neighbor, and nothing more you can give him, you've got to give yourself."

That was what she was trying to do in her letter. Unfortunately, each word was contradicted by the photo that came with it. I know she wants to help me; I feel her loving purpose —but it is hopeless from the outset. Her letter sounds a little like the farewell of a will; I have only to gaze on the picture of her calm happiness—the hat, those gloves (gloves, Irina, kidskin gloves!)—to know that my Irina is dead and that I survive alone.

I wonder sometimes whether you don't think things have been easier for me, because I am Finnish. But it is not easy to live; not for anyone. It is true that I have come to love my own freedom to the point where I felt a little sorrow at binding myself to Wieland. It's true that I learned to rebuild my nest everywhere, anywhere—in Paris, in London, in New York, in Canada, in Munich; and that I have not had a hot meal in my own home for more than ten years! Sometimes I do not even know what language I am speaking; all of them are more familiar to me than my mother tongue. I was born Finnish, I have been American, I shall die German, and it makes no difference to me. But now I can confess to you, because now I am finally admitting it to myself: it has been hard sometimes.

Remember that I was raised by my mother, like all the girls in the world, and that my mother was a strict Lutheran. She did not forgive me my liaison with Clarke. She died during the war, and I shall never know if she forgave me. My nostalgia died with her. Once you have killed your own mother within yourself, you can kill everything else; nothing else is so terrible.

Not even killing your own love. When I left Clarke, it was necessary. Precisely because I loved him. How beautiful he was! God! do you remember how beautiful Clarke was? His drug was soaking into me through the flesh that was our only bond. One step more, one day more perhaps, and I was lost for good. I ripped him from me as I had to; with a single sharp wrench, horribly brutal. The way you tear off a fingernail—and the flesh underneath

206

is pure wound. After that I could bear anything. I could even live alone. Can you? That is the whole question, and only you can answer it.

What I am about to say to you will seem very cruel, now that I have married Wieland. But as long as you do not know how to live alone, you do not know how to live. As long as you speak of men as you spoke of your husband—as an obstacle or a bridge between you and the world; until you understand that the world is given you with no intermediary—you will not be free. When I met Wieland, a year after losing Clarke, I expected nothing more from life but the very gift of life itself, and that seemed enough. The rest was given me as a bonus.

But then, even then, do you think it was all easy? Do you know what I lived? Would you be prepared to live it? Would you be prepared for all of it? I regret nothing, but I have known it all. I have known what it is to arrive at a foreign hospital, valise in hand, for a lonely miscarriage; and Christmas Eves without a letter or a gift. I learned the exhausting rhythm of long-term adultery: to die in the arms of a man every night for a week, and then live without him for a whole long year. . . . I have known a great many other things, too. Believe me or not, Sylvestre—sometimes I envied you.

If you choose freedom, you must know this: it is the toughest discipline, the heaviest armor; and it's not surprising that so many independent, emancipated women wait more or less consciously for the moment when they can give over their responsibility in a man's arms. I have lived everywhere, I have almost always lived alone, and I have not known many single women who were happy. The American women are not happy either. And the reason is that they have not yet made their choice. Like you. They want to be midnight lovers and daylight careerists both; they want independence and protection at once; they want to reconcile love and a profession; bear children and projects. You must get out of that dilemma, that double game—you must, at whatever cost. If you do go to South America, go without secret hopes! Imagining yourself closer to your cousin Costa because he is in New York is

207

an illusion. And if you marry Champell, do it in good faith—having given up Augustin in the very depth of your heart.

I am ashamed to have written you all this, because I am writing it on a pinewood table that still smells of the forest, in an inn like a color etching—a porcelain stove, a bell tower, geraniums; because Wieland is walking along the road, with a romantic cape over his shoulders; and because the sound of an accordion is floating around me. I am ashamed because I am happy, at last. I realize as I close this letter that it will be absolutely no help to you, and I love you enough to regret my happiness for a moment.

Her letter came on the morning of the day Höberlin had set. I read it and reread it. She's right: it is absolutely no help.

Even about herself Irina is telling me nothing new. I always sensed the gasp of a secret struggle in her silences. She has triumphed over everything because she had renounced everything to begin with—fine. But what counts from now on for me is that she did triumph (over her past, over Clarke, over herself, and—it's got to be acknowledged—over poor Ursula as well). I am glad for her, but her victory leaves me alone. The page we were reading together has turned. "Believe me or not, Sylvestre—sometimes I envied you." I believe you, Irina. Now I believe you.

This time I am truly alone. I am hung in space as you were; I am become a sea bird in my turn. All lone women are sea birds; they can rest only on shifting sands, and there is no port for them.

Oh, Irina, my youth, you may forget, too, that only a certain quality of solitude permits a certain quality of greatness. Perhaps I will envy you, too, in turn. It is over now for you. You passed through the doors of your Bavarian inn and the baroque church, and you left outside your rough uniform and

208

the armor of a brave, solitary woman. And now, from under the brim of your flowered hat, I see your eyes asking if I will take over the burden. See, I was right: there really is only one allotment of happiness for every two people—in all friendships, in all loves, and in each couple. We can share nothing. My faraway friendship could do nothing ever for you. Your present happiness can do nothing more for me. I read only one thing in your letter—that it is up to me to fill the place you have left empty now.

It is probably just as well, too, that Augustin never answered me. Now I can make my decision with total freedom, and that is what a human being worthy of the name must do: decide freely from a condition of total abandonment. That will have been my last weakness—waiting for word from Augustin, hoping to find him again, in a way, by traveling to another continent. And, well disguised under my love, it was my oldest weakness, too, that would have found delicious sanctuary in lying at a man's feet. True courage—and thus the true human destiny—lies in seeking out by oneself one's reasons for living. It is in receiving the world's great currents without an intermediary; it is in offering oneself without intermediary to Joy. And if there comes the companion promised each of us by Nature and the Word, then he will grasp a free hand, he will enter an open heart, he will possess a conscious living flesh.

It is one year, to the day, since I came back from Corsica and ate my first lone woman's meal from a tray near the radio. I am leaning now from this apparently motionless balcony, and attempting to gauge how far I have come.

The day is soft.... The women have all come back from their vacations now. As they pass, their low-cut dresses show their skin still tanned from the summer. Is every low neckline a wound? Is each dress a gauze bandage over a flesh stripped like a wrenched-off fingernail? No, many of these women seem happy; many are young, and some of them are beautiful. I can see the gold wedding bands shining on their hands like crowns. But I am no longer fooled by appearances; I have crossed to the other side of the wall, I belong to the kingdom of hard truths: the statistics are official, and the figures haunt me.

Out of every three of these Frenchwomen one is alone. Out of every four Frenchmen one is a Communist. Out of every three men in the world one is a Chinese. Out of every two men in the world one is hungry. Out of every two living persons one is a child under fifteen.... To be a well-fed western woman, to be one of those privileged women who I could become again tomorrow—that is not the world's truth. It is a truth, too, but a partial one, and it is under threat. The future truth is in the rising tide of peoples who we are not, in the social equalization that is brewing, and in the future of the million children who paw the ground as they wait for our deaths.

Once one has become aware of these simple essential truths —I mean vitally, constantly aware, as my forced breach with the past has made me—can one conceivably become like everyone else again? Like the minority world I belonged to? Can one simply go back to being a privileged person again? Can one agree to falling asleep again?

Then, curiously, is it up to me to go farther than Irina, farther than Augustin on the path they hewed out before me, the path where they have abandoned me? But can I? Can I? I don't know yet. In all good faith, I do not know. It is hard to refuse the delicious lie of security—and the delicious dream of sleep.

I reflected for another few hours. No, I did not reflect. Actually, I knew all along what I would do. But now it must be done very quickly.

I phoned Höberlin. That was the first miracle, it seemed to me—that my minister was so easy to reach, so available. I announced my decision. He let a long silence build between us. Finally I heard his voice, and for the first time there was not the slightest hint of banter in it.

"You've given it full consideration, I hope, Costa? If I wire Cordobal it's irrevocable. Because I bear the responsibility for your decision from now on."

"I won't change my mind."

"Well, then, my heartiest congratulations!"

"But you're the one I owe everything. Thank you, Georges; you've helped me a great deal."

I heard his unpleasant laugh. And under that laugh, which I have always loathed, I heard something a little uncomfortable, almost humble—I realized that it was the first time I had ever said a friendly word to him in so many, so very many years! Did he perhaps always feel himself ugly, too, when I looked at him? Does he feel more warmly toward me than I had always thought? No one, really—no one had ever helped me as much as my old enemy. Again I said, "Thank you, old George!"

That was all, and it was too much—he hung up immediately, muttering, "That Costa, with her fancy phrases!"

When I laid down the receiver, I heaved one of those huge sighs they say rise from relief; I say they mean physical pleasure instead.

I drank some water. A good deal of water. Then I returned to the balcony. The day was already slipping into evening, toward sleep's temptation, which is to me the greatest of all temptations. But that red sun lying on the horizon like a sick heart soon to cease its beating—that sun was already rising on the other side of the world. What importance is there, after all, to time or place? Day is everywhere the same sun. Night is always the same sleep. Sun—sleep—away—sleep. . . . It all jumbles and merges like a twirling top's colors, and the only certainty is that rest in the end. That eternal rest. . . .

For a moment I thought I was falling asleep, hanging there on the balcony; then I remembered that I had to write to Martin. And then answer Irina, and call off my meeting with Bergieri; write Mother, and Jean-Christophe. And then— But it's true! life goes on, life does begin again! That's curious, too: whatever choice we make, it is translated by a series of little acts, by an aggregation of little things. Life is a very small thing. Ultimately only death is purely great in its irreversible truth.

After all, to belong to a declining generation, to a condemned class, to a threatened country, may be as good a way as any—just a little quicker—of moving with the rest of humanity toward the single necessary end.